To the Stars, Isabelle

BY LAURENCE YEP

*To Jamie Guan for letting me watch him put his choreography together,
to Edward Gorey for his dancing cats, and, of course, to Victoria Tseng*

Published by American Girl Publishing
Copyright © 2014 American Girl

Questions or comments? Call 1-800-845-0005, visit **americangirl.com**, or write to
Customer Service, American Girl, 8400 Fairway Place, Middleton, WI 53562-0497.

Printed in China
14 15 16 17 18 19 20 21 LEO 10 9 8 7 6 5 4 3 2 1

Illustrations by Anna Kmet

Special thanks to Kristy Callaway, executive director of Arts Schools Network;
and Shannon Gallagher, owner of and instructor at Premier Dance Academy, LLC,
Madison, WI

Cataloging-in-Publication Data available from the Library of Congress.

Contents

Chapter 1: Flowers and Pirates....................1

Chapter 2: The Captain's Baton...................10

Chapter 3: A Sea Fairy.......................... 25

Chapter 4: Costumes and Capes...................41

Chapter 5: Dancing with a Butterfly.............. 58

Chapter 6: The Pig-Hat Party 70

Chapter 7: A Bad Case of Nerves................ 83

Chapter 8: A Very Special Guest................. 94

Chapter 9: Hugging the Moon................... 111

Real Girls, Real Stories..........................119

Now I knew how it felt to be an only child—to be without my big sister, Jade. It felt *lousy*.

Jade had deserted me, so I was all by myself as I got off the city bus on Saturday morning. It didn't help my mood any that the bus had been running late. Clutching the strap of my dance bag, I hurried toward our school, Anna Hart School of the Arts.

It had been so great when my idol, Jackie Sanchez, invited me to join a special project of hers—a spring dance tour. I mean, how often does a ten-year-old girl get to work with a world-class ballerina? Jackie was not only a principal dancer at New York City Ballet but had been a guest artist in some of the best ballet companies around the world. And to think, she'd started out at Anna Hart, just like me.

Jackie had convinced our school to put together a show from some of our Autumn Festival acts and to let our tour group use the school for rehearsals every Saturday. We'd perform five weeks from now, during spring vacation. It was an amazing opportunity, so I'd been shocked when Jade turned down Jackie's invitation. But Jade explained that if she wanted to join a ballet company, she had to perfect her technique. To do that, she'd begun taking private lessons on the weekend. That meant Jade had no time for rehearsals with Jackie—and barely any time to hang out with me anymore.

How am I going to do this without Jade? I wondered. When I was having problems with my dancing for the Autumn Festival, she had saved me with some good advice. She had also helped me while we were rehearsing for *The Nutcracker* with the HDC—the Hart Dance Company. But then, ever since I was little, Jade had been like a fairy godmother, coming to my rescue whenever I was in trouble.

Well, I thought sadly, *maybe you wore her out.*

At least my friends and classmates Luisa and Gabriel would be with me. Jackie had liked Luisa's pirate routine at the Autumn Festival, and when she was looking for a master of ceremonies to entertain the audience between acts, I'd thought right away of Gabriel. Between his sense of humor and his magic tricks, he could entertain any crowd.

Jackie Sanchez had asked Gabriel, Luisa, and me to be in her show, and she'd asked only *six* others. That thought made me feel so lucky and happy that I spun a couple of times along the sidewalk.

There was Gabriel now, sitting on the front steps of our school. He was wearing a red, white, and blue Washington Nationals jacket in honor of his favorite baseball team. His backpack was by his feet, and his usual deck of playing cards was in his hand. He could make those cards do almost anything.

"Why aren't you inside?" I asked. "It's nine o'clock already."

"I was waiting for you or Luisa," he said as a half-dozen cards sprayed from his fingers.

Gabriel's hands were usually so strong and sure. As I helped him pick up the cards, I asked, "Are you nervous?"

He nodded as he tucked the cards back into the deck. "Aren't you?" he asked.

"A little," I admitted.

Gabriel slid the cards into his pocket. "Well, we should be," he said. "I mean, this is *Jackie Sanchez*. I don't know whether to be glad or mad that you recommended me to her."

I had met Jackie before, during rehearsals for *The Nutcracker*, and she'd given me some good advice about shaking off mistakes during performances. "She's really nice," I said, trying to sound casual. "Don't worry."

Our footsteps echoed in the hallway as we entered the school. I shuffled a little closer to Gabriel.

"Do you think this building's really haunted?"

3

I asked. The old part of our school dated back to the nineteenth century, when it had been used as a Civil War hospital.

"Nah, I don't believe all that. Do you?" Gabriel asked.

"Well, it's a little spooky when it's empty like this," I said and almost jumped when the front door creaked open and then crashed shut again. I was glad to see it wasn't a ghost—it was Luisa. She was wearing a brown jacket over her red sweater, looking like the first robin of spring.

"Oh, good," Luisa said when she saw us. "I'm not late."

"No, you're late," Gabriel said with a grin. "But you've got good company."

We started jogging down the hallway into the modern annex of the school. From up ahead, we could hear voices talking, muffled by the walls into a high-pitched buzzing sound, like bees being tickled.

When Gabriel opened the door to the ballet studio, I saw five or six kids sitting on the floor—all of them grinning and shifting restlessly with excitement. I recognized Jacob and Saafi, who had gotten big laughs at the Autumn Festival in their act from *The Merry Wives of Windsor*. Ryan, a sixth-grade violinist, was chatting with another sixth-grader, Hailey, who had a great singing voice.

Sitting cross-legged in front of them was my classmate Olivia, who had danced with me in "The Waltz of the Flowers." She smiled and picked up her bag so that we could sit next to her.

But I saw Renata sitting just beyond Olivia, twisting around to show off her bracelet to Saafi. Renata was a classmate who really knew how to get under my skin. So I waved a hand at Olivia to come join us instead. She glanced at Renata and nodded her head in understanding before standing up and grabbing her bag.

We had barely sat down when Jackie Sanchez walked in. The studio fell silent, and everyone sat up a little straighter.

Jackie was a tall, olive-skinned woman who walked with the confidence of someone who is used to being onstage. Her braided hair was pulled into a bun at the base of her neck, and she wore a lavender top with loose blue warm-up pants.

With her was Ms. Hawken, my ballet teacher, who had taught us the Waltzing Flowers routine. Three other teachers filed into the room behind her: Ms. Steinberg, a drama teacher; Mr. Leonard, a vocal arts teacher; and Ms. Teasdale, a strings teacher.

"Hello," Jackie called out to us in a pleasant voice. "I want to thank you all for coming this morning and for embarking on this adventure with me."

I saw heads turning as students smiled at one another. This definitely felt like the beginning of something special.

Jackie spread her hands and said, "There are plenty of people who would have loved to see your Autumn Festival but couldn't. Maybe they were recovering from illness or injury, or they're elderly and have trouble getting around. That's why for three days during spring vacation, we're going to bring your show to nursing homes and hospitals so that those people can enjoy it too."

Jackie smiled encouragingly and went on. "Each of you represents the very best of Anna Hart's talent and generous spirit. But because the Autumn Festival was many months ago, you'll need to knock the rust off. We'll have to rehearse like crazy for the next few Saturdays."

The faces around me suddenly looked nervous, but what Jackie said made sense. We had to get back our timing. Smaller dance casts also meant we'd have to change up the staging and choreography.

"And since we'll be a touring company, you're not going to have sets," Jackie said. Then she began to tick off other items on her fingers. "No lighting system. And the sound system will be pared down to the bone. We won't be dancing on our usual wood floors, and the size of our 'stage' will change from location to location. We may even be performing in noisy public spaces with lots of distractions. We'll have to be real troupers who depend on one another."

Heads swiveled in the studio, and kids began to talk in low, worried voices.

Jackie raised her hand to reassure us. "But I guarantee that every one of you will grow as an artist," she said. "Because it'll just be you and the audience—people who really need to see your talent and the joy you feel when you're performing." She let those words sink in and then asked, "Any questions?" The room was silent.

When it was time to split up and start rehearsing, Jacob and Saafi left with their drama teacher, Ms. Steinberg. Hailey headed to another classroom with her vocal teacher, Mr. Leonard, while Ryan went with Ms. Teasdale to the music room.

"Waltzing Flowers—Renata and Olivia—please stay here with Ms. Hawken," Jackie said. "Gabriel, why don't you watch the flower routine today, too, so you'll get ideas for how to introduce it during the show." Then she motioned me and Luisa toward the door. "Isabelle, grab your bag and come along with Luisa and me."

Did she think I was a pirate like Luisa? "B-but I'm a flower, not a pirate," I said.

There were a couple of giggles at that. Even I had to admit it sounded funny.

"I talked with Mr. Amici," Jackie said, "and he said you'd learned the pirate routine in his modern dance class. I thought Luisa could use your company and skills. What do you say?"

I hesitated. I'd enjoyed learning the pirate routine in class, but it would be a lot different performing it before an audience.

Renata twisted around and smirked at me. She was enjoying seeing me squirm.

Don't let her get to you again, I told myself. *Ignore her, just like you did during rehearsals for* The Nutcracker. *Besides, if Mr. Amici thinks you can do it, then you can.*

"Okay. I'll be a pirate," I announced, with more confidence than I actually felt. It was all I could do to keep from making a face back at Renata.

"Argh, welcome aboard, matey," Luisa growled.

Jackie smiled and started for the door.
"Great! Let's get going then, girls," she called to us.

Renata began waving her arm frantically.
"Jackie, aren't you going to work with the Waltzing
Flowers, too?" she asked.

"I am," Jackie said, "but Ms. Hawken knows
your flower routine better than I do. And since Mr.
Amici can't be here, I'll be covering for him with the
pirates. But don't worry. Ms. Hawken will record your
rehearsals for me to watch later, and we'll put our
heads together on your staging."

Renata opened her mouth to protest, but
Ms. Hawken cut her off. "For now, you'll have to put
up with just me, Renata," Ms. Hawken said pleasantly
but firmly. "Let's get started."

In a daze, I gathered up my stuff. I'd never
expected to be working with Jackie almost one on
one, especially on the pirate dance. Would I be able to
live up to her standards? Luisa looked just as scared
as I felt. She raised her eyebrows at me as we followed
Jackie out the door and down the long hall.

"This sure brings back memories," Jackie said, slowing to a stroll as we entered the old building. She glanced through the open doors of classrooms as we passed. Was she remembering the classes she took when she was a student here, like me?

When Jackie stepped inside the modern dance studio, she walked over to a corner and crouched down to examine one of the mirrored walls. "The crack's still there," she said, sounding pleased.

Even though I was feeling shy, I asked, "What crack?"

Jackie tapped a teeny flaw on the mirror. "Mr. Amici and I were improvising together in class, and we got a little carried away," she said. "He accidentally kicked the wall."

"You took modern dance from him?" Luisa asked.

"He was one of the best teachers I ever had," Jackie said, straightening back up. "He was lucky he didn't break any bones when he hit that mirror." She chuckled. "But he did limp for a while. And he likes to brag that if he could survive teaching me, he can survive any student."

Luisa and I grinned at each other. We dumped our things in a corner and began warming up.

I couldn't help sneaking peeks at Jackie, who was stretching alongside us. She was so flexible!

Jackie caught me watching her. "Don't look so surprised, Isabelle," she said, smiling. "I practice almost every day."

"Really?" Luisa said, grunting a little as she leaned forward.

"There's always some new challenge in ballet for me," Jackie said. "After all these years, I feel like I'm still learning."

That left me feeling a little uncomfortable. If an experienced dancer like Jackie felt that way, what hope was there for a student like me?

Jackie lay on her back and stretched her leg overhead. "That's how you tell a real dancer from someone who's just posing as one," she explained. "The real dancer wants to get better each day."

My dad had once told me almost the same thing. Both of my parents said they still learned something from each new project—my mom with her textile art and my dad with his music. I wished I could focus, too, on just learning something new. But right now, all I could think about was not messing up in front of my idol.

When Jackie thought we were stretched and

ready, she took out her phone and sat down in the middle of the floor. "Come sit by me," she said. "I'd like you both to refresh your memory."

When Luisa and I had taken seats on either side of Jackie, she laughed. "Come in closer," she said, patting the floor. "I won't bite—much."

Luisa and I giggled nervously as we inched in closer to Jackie, and she held up her phone so that we could see the screen. "Mr. Amici sent me this video of one of your rehearsals," she said, pushing the play button.

Very faintly, as if performed by elves, the tinny notes of the pirate music began to play. It was only about three minutes long with a half minute for the full cast to dance together at the beginning and the end. The middle two minutes were a contest between the pirates over who was the best dancer. Each pirate had ten seconds to dance a solo.

"All right," Jackie said as the video ended. "We'll keep the choreography for the beginning and the ending. But since there are only two of you, your solo dances will be longer—a minute or so. And you're the last act of the show, so your performances have really got to make the audience feel alive."

I swallowed hard. It would be tough enough to

perfect a new, sixty-second modern dance solo. It was even scarier to think that it had to be good enough to serve as the grand finale. I stole a nervous glance at Luisa, who was chewing her lip.

"Let's rehearse the first part," Jackie said as she rose. "Luisa, you know this the best, so you take the lead."

Having Jackie Sanchez watch us made my nerves feel all jangly. But when she docked her phone and music began to play from the studio speakers, the practice in all those modern dance classes took over. My body performed the first few moves all on its own. Luisa and I launched into what Mr. Amici called the *hornpipe*, an old sailor dance made up of movements such as "looking out to sea" with our hands raised to our foreheads, and hopping on one leg like a boat bobbing on water.

Luisa completed the routine easily, but my own timing was a little off, and every once in a while I forgot a move and had to watch Luisa.

Still, Jackie was pleased. "Good. Now let's use more of the stage. Luisa, start in the center, and Isabelle, you'll be here," she said, positioning me to the right and behind Luisa. From this new position, I could mimic my friend's moves more easily.

We danced the routine a few more times, and Jackie adjusted the staging and steps after each. I was starting to think that *maybe* I could handle this—until Jackie said it was time to start working on our solos.

"For your solos, I want . . ." She opened and closed her fingers several times, as if trying to grasp something. "I want your joy to be *bursting* out of you as you dance," she finally said.

I waited for her to give us our choreography, but instead she said, "We'll start with improvs." She glanced down at her belongings and then unclipped a butterfly charm from the strap of her dance bag. "This'll do," she said. "Let's call it the 'captain's baton.' Whoever holds it can make up a short set of steps. The other person has to imitate those steps and also add something. If I think she does so successfully, I'll tell *her* to take the baton."

"So she becomes the captain and decides on the next set?" Luisa asked.

"Exactly," said Jackie, putting the butterfly charm in Luisa's hand. "You can do your favorite moves from any kind of dance—ballet, Irish jig, hip-hop, tap, you name it." She fiddled with her phone. "I've put the pirate-routine music on continuous loop, so just keep dancing."

As the first notes of the techno-pop song began to play, Luisa glanced at me nervously. I was feeling just as anxious. It was one thing to improvise for a teacher like Mr. Amici, but another thing altogether to do it for Jackie Sanchez. What if we messed up? Would Jackie think she had made a mistake inviting us to be a part of her show?

Spreading her arms, Luisa took several steps, paused, and raised one leg behind her. As she whipped the leg down, she launched into a pirouette. Then, shifting her weight from one leg to the other, she swung her clasped hands back and forth as she wriggled her shoulders.

Luisa's steps were straight out of her pirate routine, and I had no problem imitating them. But I couldn't figure out what to add at the end, so I just spread my fingers and shook my palms.

"Luisa wins," Jackie announced. "Isabelle, you've got to do more than jazz hands."

I felt my ears burn. Worse than doing something silly, I'd done something "blah." Mr. Amici sometimes said that "the biggest mistake a dancer can make is to be dull, dull, dull." If I kept this up, I'd put Jackie to sleep.

Luisa stayed cautious for the next two turns,

again doing stuff from the pirate routine. I was just as careful when I added my own moves. I did a few steps from my Waltzing Flowers choreography, but I kept them simple because I was afraid of making a mistake.

After three consecutive victories, though, Luisa was feeling pretty good about herself. She pursed her lips thoughtfully for a moment and then smiled wickedly. Shifting her weight from one leg to another, she began to sway her shoulders and move them up and down.

"Hey, no fair," I said. "You're samba-ing."

"The steps can come from any style of dance," Jackie reminded me.

Luisa began to move her feet rapidly. If she'd been dancing to real samba music, I probably couldn't have followed what she did. Her family is Brazilian and her father is a musician, so she's been dancing the samba all her life. But she had to slow down to the tempo of the pirate tune, so I could see every step she made. She finished with a pirouette.

And that was her mistake.

I'd done a bunch of pirouettes in my routine for *The Nutcracker*, so I was pretty good at them now. After I mimicked Luisa's samba, I pictured a toy top in my mind as I spun once, twice, three times in near-perfect pirouettes.

"Isabelle wins," Jackie announced. "She's the new captain."

Yes! I felt like taking a victory lap around the studio.

With a shrug, Luisa handed me the baton—the butterfly charm. It was warm from her hand.

"Really try to think of something new this time, Isabelle," Jackie urged.

Safely clutching the baton, I thought for a moment. *What would a pirate do?* Then I thought of my dad's favorite old-time pirate movie—so old that it had been filmed in black and white.

I smiled and struck a pose, standing on one leg while crossing the other in front. With one hand on my hip, I raised the other in a casual salute. Shifting my feet into the position for a *jeté*, I put up my hands as if I were holding on to a rope. Then I kicked off with all the energy I could muster, leaping into the air.

Jade always said that leaps were one of my best skills as a dancer. So when I landed, I kicked off again, moving across the studio as if leaping from the deck of one ship to another. I ended by focusing on my other strength: I launched into a few pirouettes as

I waved an imaginary sword over my head.

"Good, Isabelle!" Jackie called, just as Luisa began copying my routine. She did all the moves successfully and finished with a high kick. Luisa was a good leaper, but not as good as me, so I kept the captain's baton.

Before we began the next round, though, Jackie had some advice for us. "You're both holding your breath when you jump," she pointed out, "and that makes you a little stiff. You need to keep breathing during your jetés."

Luisa and I each tried an experimental jump, focusing on our breath, and it *did* feel easier. I couldn't believe Jackie had helped me improve one of my strongest moves with such a simple tip! *I want to learn everything I can from her,* I thought happily as I tried another leap.

Luisa and I traded the baton back and forth so many times that I lost count. We were both laughing by the time Jackie turned off the music.

"Let's take a breather," she said.

Luisa leaned forward and rested her hands on her knees. Panting, I glanced at the clock in the studio.

I was surprised to see that rehearsal was almost over.

"That was good," Jackie said. "I really saw your joy while you danced, girls." She curved her back as she stretched and then sighed. "I haven't had this much fun in a long time."

Neither have I, I realized suddenly. I'd been so nervous before rehearsal started, but now I was having the time of my life. I didn't want the morning to end!

As Jackie reattached the butterfly charm to her bag, she said, "That game was a big help to me. Between Mr. Amici's choreography and your improvs today, I've got enough ideas to come up with two good solos for you."

I blinked. I thought the improvs had been a warm-up. Was Jackie really going to create routines for us based on our made-up moves?

Jackie must have seen the confusion on my face, because she said, "A lot of choreographers base their dances on what they see their dancers create and on the moves they do best."

That made sense, and it was exciting to think that Jackie was going to use some of the moves we had come up with. It was as if we were her creative partners. "Do you want more?" I asked with a glance toward Luisa. "We could dance another round."

Luisa shrugged. "Sure, why not?"

"I love your enthusiasm!" Jackie said, laughing. "You'll need to call on that joyful energy when you perform in the show. Your grand finale really has to wow the audience—to make sure that they have as much fun as you're having while you dance."

I thought about our future audiences—sick children and other patients at hospitals. Suddenly I had an idea.

As the words started rolling off my tongue, it was hard for me to stop them. "My dad works as an administrator at a hospital, and sometimes I go with him to visit the children's ward. We take along a 'fun box' full of costumes and props so that the kids can dress up," I said. "Maybe we could get the kids in our audiences involved if we bring along something like that!"

Jackie's smile lit up the studio. "Yes, we could turn the whole show into a kind of costume party," she said, sweeping her palm in an arc through the air. "We'll call it the 'Big Hart Party.' How fun! I knew I could count on you for fresh ideas, Isabelle."

"I bet my dad would loan us his box," I said, pride and excitement swelling in my chest.

"Yes, and all the performers could distribute

props from the box," said Jackie excitedly. Then she paused. "Hmm. But you'll all be in different costumes. It'd be nice if we had some visual cue to tie all of you together at the start and maybe at the end."

Suddenly I had another brainstorm. "How about capes?" I asked.

"Yes, I like that! Where would we get so many capes on such short notice, though?" Jackie asked.

"I could ask my mom to help," I said. My mom is an amazing seamstress who often helps sew costumes for our dance productions.

Jackie wrinkled her forehead. "Wait, slow down for a minute. You're going to need a new costume for the pirate routine, aren't you?" she asked. "Your mom will most likely be busy enough with that."

"We can come up with something and still do the capes," I promised. "I . . . I usually help my mom a lot with the designing and sewing." It felt funny telling Jackie that. I didn't want her to think I was bragging, but I knew that if we worked together, my mom and I could get the job done.

"Isabelle is a really talented designer," Luisa piped up. "She helped design some of the costumes for *The Nutcracker.*"

I shifted uncomfortably at Luisa's praise.

"Is that right? That's great to hear, Isabelle, and I do like your cape idea," Jackie said. "But focus on your costume first, and then we can see about the capes, okay? And as you think about that pirate costume, steer clear of the usual pirate clichés." She fluttered a hand near her throat. "You know, no frilly shirts or coats with lots of braid."

Jackie looked out the window as a new thought occurred to her. "In fact, let's think outside the box for your character," she said. "Perhaps you're not even a pirate at all. Maybe you're another character inspired by the sea. What do you think?"

It was Luisa who answered, almost proudly, "Isabelle will come up with something special. She always does."

I felt myself stand a little taller then, rising to the challenge.

When Jackie dismissed us at the end of practice, Luisa and I started to do a *reverence*—a curtsy done as a way to thank ballet teachers at the end of class. But Jackie waved for us to stop.

"We're shipmates now," she said, holding out her index finger like a sword.

I stared at it, puzzled, but then Luisa put her

own index finger over Jackie's finger. "Shipmates," she repeated.

I rested my finger on top of theirs. "Shipmates."

Jackie's hand dipped and then rose several times, taking our hands with it, and then we broke apart. I didn't think any pirate had had an adventure as special as this—it was scary and wonderful and fun, all at the same time.

As we left the studio, we met the Waltzing Flowers in the hallway. Ms. Hawken must have just let them out, too.

"So, what's Jackie like?" Olivia demanded eagerly.

"She's really nice," I said.

"Well, duh, of course she's nice," Renata snapped. She looked envious that we had spent so much time with Jackie. "She organized this tour, after all."

"She doesn't act like a star at all," Luisa said. "She's just a regular person."

"What did she have you do?" Olivia asked.

"We played an improv game where we danced like pirates and tried to outdo each other," I said, grinning at Luisa as I remembered how much fun we'd had.

"And next week we'll learn solo routines she'll create for us based on our own best moves," Luisa added proudly.

From the corner of my eye, I saw Renata. I wished I had a photo of her face at that moment. She looked as if she had just sucked on a whole basketful of lemons.

When I walked through our front door a little after noon, I immediately started shouting for my sister. "Jade!" I was bursting with all the great stuff that had just happened, and I wanted to share it with her.

When she didn't answer right away, I tried again. She'd had private lessons early this morning, but she should have been back by now. When she still didn't respond, I yelled, "Mom? Dad?"

But there was only silence in the house, not even a mew from Tutu.

I headed into the kitchen. My family led such busy lives that we used the fridge as our bulletin board. That's when I saw the note:

We went to the Mall to find inspiration for Jade's school report. We'll be back by 1:00 for lunch. Text me when you get home, and remember that Mrs. Ordway is next door if you need her.

Love, Mom

There was only one "mall" for Mom, and that was the National Mall. It had nothing to do with shopping. The National Mall was the long grassy area stretching from the Lincoln Memorial to the Capitol Building. The Mall was surrounded by museums, from the National Gallery of Art to the original brick Smithsonian Institution to the Air and Space Museum.

I pulled out my phone and sent off a quick text to Mom. I felt a little sad that my family had gone without me. But that had been my choice, after all. I was the one who had decided to do the tour.

The sound of my footsteps in the kitchen brought our curious cat, Tutu, to the doorway. "At least you didn't desert me," I said as I scooped her up into my arms. "I had the *best* day, Tutu. It was like having my own master class with Jackie Sanchez." A *master class* is a lesson that a famous artist might give, and I couldn't think of a more amazing instructor than Jackie.

Tutu began licking her shoulder.

"You could at least *pretend* to listen," I grumbled.

I had to work off my extra energy somehow, so I hugged Tutu close to my chest and started to dance a hornpipe around the kitchen, skipping first on one leg and then on the other. For a while, Tutu let me cradle her in my arms, but she quickly got fed up and jumped to the floor.

With my hands on my hips, I danced after her, hopping along and kicking my feet in the air. At first,

A Sea Fairy

Tutu tried to keep a dignified pace down the hallway, her tail pointing straight up like a flag. But the steady thumping finally got to her. Poor Tutu broke into a run toward the living room. My last sight of her was her tail disappearing under the sofa.

I was feeling very sailor-like as I skipped around the living room, pretending to haul up an anchor cable and climb the riggings of masts. Finally, panting and laughing, I fell onto the sofa.

My whole body was tired, but dancing for my idol had made me too excited to rest. Even if my arms and legs were finally still, my mind went on racing.

When my stomach growled, I pulled myself up off the couch and got a banana from the kitchen. I ate it in the living room and started thinking about my costume. Possibilities whirled through my head. I sat up suddenly to reach for my tablet, which lay on the coffee table, and began to sketch out ideas.

I was still drawing when I heard the front door open. "We're home," Dad called.

"Ahoy from the living room!" I shouted back.

I heard the rustle of coats as my family hung them up on the hooks by the doorway, and then they trooped into the living room.

"How'd it—?" Jade began to ask, but I'd already jumped up and grabbed her.

"It was crazy, crazy fun!" I said as I began to spin her around the room.

She let me whirl her around for a minute and then put her hands on my shoulders. "Whoa. I can see that," she said, laughing.

Mom settled onto the sofa beside Dad. "What happened, honey? Tell us!" she said.

I let go of Jade and wheeled around to face my parents. "Guess what I'm going to be?" I said mysteriously. But I couldn't wait to tell them. "I'm going to be a pirate!"

"Oh, I know the perfect costume for you then," said Jade. She fluttered her hand excitedly beneath her throat. "A shirt with lots of lace"—she gestured toward a shoulder—"and a coat with shiny gold stuff on the shoulders."

I shook my head. "Jackie already told me she wants something different from a normal pirate costume," I said.

Jade looked skeptical. "When did you get a chance to talk to her about your outfit?" she asked.

"I worked with her all *morning*," I bragged.

"Really?" Mom said in amazement.

"That's incredible, honey," said Dad, giving me a high five.

"She's already taught me something new," I said eagerly. "I mean, I thought my jetés were pretty good."

"They are," Jade said confidently.

"Well, Jackie noticed that I was holding my breath when I jumped," I said. "It's such a small thing, but it made a big difference when I tried it again and focused on my breathing."

"Huh, I've got to remember that," Jade said thoughtfully.

I went on, reliving the wonderful morning. "We played this game where Luisa and I had to copy each other's dance steps and then make up new ones," I said, explaining all about the improvs and what we each had done to try to win the captain's baton.

"Wow," Jade said, sounding sorry that she hadn't come with me after all.

"But that's not all," I said, pausing for effect. "Jackie's going to use some of the moves we made up to create solos for each of us."

Jade looked stunned. "She's choreographing a routine for you?" she said, eyes wide. "Do you know how many people would love to be in your shoes?"

I remembered Renata's face as we left the school. *I know of one,* I thought to myself with a satisfied smile.

"Hey, maybe Jackie will want to hear this joke," Dad said, clapping a hand over one eye. "Argh, matey, why did the sailor paint an 'X' on his dog?"

Jade rolled her eyes and frowned at me. "It's your fault for giving him that joke book for Christmas," she murmured.

"Give up yet?" Dad asked with a sly grin.

I raised my hands in surrender. "Okay, Dad, why did the sailor paint his dog?" I asked.

"Because 'X' marks the Spot," Dad said, and he began laughing.

Mom patted Dad on the shoulder. "All right, dear," she said gently. "That's your quota of jokes for the day."

Dad lowered his hand, disappointed. "I'm just getting started," he protested.

Mom held up an index finger. "One," she said firmly.

I was eager to tell them more about my session with Jackie Sanchez, but I thought I should be polite. "How was the Mall?" I asked.

A Sea Fairy

"Incredible," Mom said. "The National Gallery had an exhibit on how dancers have inspired art-work—from cave paintings twelve thousand years old to modern art today."

"I would've liked to have seen that," I said, whining just a little.

"You can't do *everything*, honey," Mom said. "Washington's like a three-ring circus, with some-thing spectacular going on in each ring—kind of like our lives these days." She sighed and asked, "So what's Jackie Sanchez like?"

"She doesn't act like a big star at all," I said, gushing. "And when I told her about Dad's fun box, she thought it was a great idea. Can we borrow it for the tour, Dad—to make our show feel more like a party for the kids?"

"Of course," said Dad, sounding pleased. "You'll probably want my joke book then, too."

"Uh, thanks, but I think I have enough to handle with the dancing," I said quickly. Then I turned to Mom. "And Mom, can you help me with my costume?"

She nodded. "As soon as you give me a sketch," she said.

"And could I have some fabric?" I asked.

"I thought the performers could all wear capes. Jackie loved the idea. I want to bring her a sample next week."

"Of course," Mom said.

I jumped up. "Could we start now?" I asked eagerly.

"Take it easy, Isabelle," Mom said, smiling. "Remember that going too fast leads to mistakes."

I'd definitely learned that lesson before. "Right—slow and steady, and I'll do most of the work," I promised.

We went into Mom's sewing room, where she began to pull material off shelves. "How's this?" she asked, handing me a bolt of shimmery green cloth.

I unrolled some of the fabric. I loved how it seemed to pour cool and silky smooth across my palms. "It's perfect!" I said to Mom. "But there might not be enough for all the capes."

"Don't worry. I know where I can get more," Mom said. "You cut the material for the sample cape, and I'll hem it up." Then she asked, "Have you thought about your own costume yet?"

"I've done some sketches, but so far nothing's jumped out at me," I confessed.

"I'll pull out some books to give you ideas

while you cut the cloth for the cape," said Mom, scanning the bookshelf in the corner. "Be sure to cut the cape as a trapezoid—narrower at the shoulders and wider at the bottom so that it'll really swing." She pointed to her throat. "And cut a strip for the collar, too, so that we can fasten the cape around the neck."

I found some fabric scissors and began to cut the material, making the cape long enough to reach my waist. Then I cut a strip of fabric for a collar and trimmed away the loose threads along the edges.

By then, Mom had set a stack of books on the floor. I handed the cape to her, and she sat down behind Henrietta, her trusty sewing machine. With the familiar *brrrr* of the machine in the background, I started looking at the books and tried to think about my own costume. But my mind was still stuck on the cape. As pretty as the shimmery green cloth was, it needed something more.

"Mom, can I make a design on the cape with sequins?" I asked.

Mom kept her head bent over Henrietta. "Sure. You know where the sequins are," she said. "If you baste them in place, I can sew them on later."

So I went to the shelves stacked with plastic

bins, sorting through the ones with the tiny shiny sequins until I decided on a bright magenta. I took the bin and a needle and thread over to my desk.

Now, what design should I create? I wondered, staring at the sequins. Of the many images running through my head, one leaped out at me. I'd make the sample cape for Luisa, with a design of a ship with three masts on the back. Anything less would have been an insult to a captain like her.

As I sketched the design on a piece of scrap paper, satisfaction grew inside me, as warm and comforting as the sound of Tutu purring—or the whir of Mom's sewing machine. It felt good to be working with Mom in the sewing room again.

"Here you go," Mom announced finally, holding up the hemmed cape.

"Thanks!" I said. As I studied the cape, I knew I had been right. The cape needed some sort of picture on the back of it. "I'm going to put this on it," I said, showing Mom my design.

She glanced at my sketch. "Nice," she said. "I can't wait to see it! But its way past lunchtime. I should make some food. Can you take it from here, hon?"

"Yup, I can handle this," I said.

"Okay then," she said, kissing the top of my

head before stepping out of the room.

As impatient as I was to finish the cape, I kept checking the design I was creating against my sketch to be sure it was just right. By the time I was done, yummy smells were slipping under the door from the kitchen, and my stomach began to growl.

While we sipped French onion soup for lunch, Jade told me more about the exhibit. "When I saw the Nereid there, I knew that's what I wanted to report on for my visual arts class," she said. "She was standing like this." Hopping up from her chair, she raised her arms into an arc over her head. It would have looked more graceful if Jade hadn't still been holding a soup-spoon in one hand.

"The near-what?" I asked.

"Nereid. Nereids were goddesses in Greek legends who danced with the moon," Jade explained as she danced a few steps across the kitchen floor. "Do you want to see the postcard I bought of her?"

"Sure," I said quickly. I was definitely curious about this Nereid.

Jade left the kitchen and returned a moment later to show me a painting of a girl who seemed to be hovering over a dark sea of water. She wore a short, ivory-colored dress that gleamed like the whitecaps surrounding her. She was so light that her feet barely touched the water, and as she twisted at the waist and stretched her arms upward to hug the moon, her whole body curled as gracefully as the shining ribbons of spray that rose from the waves.

"She's beautiful," I said. "She looks like a sea fairy."

"I love her smile," Jade murmured, tracing it with a finger. "She looks so happy."

As Mom, Dad, and Jade told me more about the exhibit, my eyes kept straying back to the postcard Jade had propped up against a bowl. *I wish I could dance like her,* I thought enviously.

When lunch was finished, I started stacking the plates, but Jade said, "Leave that to me."

"But it's my turn to do the dishes," I said.

"I may not be able to help with your costume," Jade said, "but I can at least give you time to work on it yourself."

"Don't you have to practice dancing?" I asked. "Or work on your school report?"

"I'll do all that later," Jade said firmly, and I could tell she meant business.

I couldn't remember the last time Jade had offered to do dishes for me, so how could I turn

her down? I *did* have to design a costume, after all,
"Thanks, sis," I said. "What would I do without you?"

Jade paused and then said, "Oh, I think you'd
be just fine." Something about her tone sounded
odd, but when I gave her a questioning look, she just
smiled and gave me a playful pat. "Get going already,
Isabelle!" she said. "You have work to do."

Because Mom's job at the Smithsonian
Institution was restoring antique textiles and
clothing, she had a lot of books on seventeenth- and
eighteenth-century fashion. I spent the afternoon
leafing through a stack of them in the sewing room,
looking at the pictures. Unfortunately, the books gave
me *too* many ideas, so before my head exploded with
pirate designs, I put the books away to look at later.

After dinner, I carefully folded the cape and
tucked it into my bag so that I could show it to Luisa
on Monday. It was only eight o'clock, but the lower
floor of our house was dark. Up above me, I could
hear the boards creaking as Dad walked around my
parents' bedroom. I heard music from the bedroom
I shared with Jade, and the rhythmic sound of her
dancing feet.

I could have gone upstairs, too, but today had felt like a piece of my favorite chocolate. I just wanted to sit somewhere by myself and remember the sweetness. So I went into the living room.

As I walked through the doorway, I created a slight breeze that made Mom's artwork, a mobile called "Pond Dreams," spin and move. Shadows danced across the floor. Traffic had thinned out on the freeway near our house, so the sound of cars came and went like the whoosh of ocean surf.

Tutu was asleep on a chair. Her fur seemed to shine like pale fire, and I realized that the light in the room was too strong to be coming from just the streetlamp outside.

I sat down, careful not to wake Tutu, and looked out the window. The full moon floated in the night sky like a pale, round lantern. Its soft light spilled across our neighbors' houses and flooded into our living room, coating everything with a silvery finish. It made everything seem strange and dreamy.

Staring up at the moon, I could see its face so clearly. It was smiling—just as I was. So I sat there for a long time, keeping it company.

"What are you looking at?" Jade asked as she came into the room and sat down beside me.

Silently, I pointed at the moon.

"Oh," Jade said softly.

I felt ribbons of moonlight curl delicately around my ankles, pulling me to my feet. The floor spread in front of me like a calm, dark sea, and the bright moon kept tugging, urging me to dance with it.

Stretching out my arms, I leaped forward, and I saw Jade rising beside me, too. As the moon wrapped its silvery light around us, I felt as weightless as the dancer on Jade's postcard.

Suddenly, I stopped dancing. "I know *just* what I want to be for the pirate routine," I whispered, as much to myself as to Jade.

"What?" Jade asked, her arms poised in midair.

"A sea fairy!" I announced happily as I spun again beneath the spotlight of the moon.

After my high-powered rehearsal with Jackie, it was nice to get back to my normal routine at school on Monday. But as soon as Jade and I entered the building, kids began to come up and ask me about Jackie.

Even Gemma, a friend of Jade's with curly brown hair, fell in step beside us and asked, "Did you really work with Jackie Sanchez one-on-one, Isabelle?"

"Well, Luisa and I both did," I answered honestly.

"This is so not fair," Gemma moaned. "Why didn't Jackie Sanchez ask *me* to be in her tour?"

It felt odd to have everyone's attention on me instead of on my sister. At first, Jade was smiling. She seemed to think the situation was funny. But as more students crowded around, she held up her wrist and tapped her watch.

"Gotta go," she said. As my sister disappeared down the hall, leaving me surrounded by a ring of admiring students, I felt as if the whole world had turned upside down.

When I finally reached my locker, Luisa was just closing her own. She seemed relieved to see me. "Have people been asking you about our rehearsal with Jackie?" she asked.

"Yeah, weird, huh?" I said. "But who told them?"

Luisa jerked her head at Gabriel, two lockers

down. "Blame Big Mouth there," she said, rolling her eyes.

Gabriel didn't look sorry at all. "Hey, if magic doesn't work out, maybe I'll get a job on one of those TV gossip shows," he joked.

Sliding my book bag off my shoulder, I set it on the floor and carefully took out the cape. "What do you think of this?" I asked my friends.

Luisa reached for the cape right away. Fastening it around her neck, she did a spin, laughing as it billowed around her. "I love it," she said.

Gabriel pointed at the ship outlined in magenta sequins on the green cloth. "Did you design that one for Luisa?" he asked. "She's really more of a shark than a ship."

Luisa made a face at him. "Well, yours should have a parrot. A real squawky one," she retorted. She folded up the cape carefully and handed it back to me.

Gabriel just laughed. "Later," he said as he headed off to class.

That afternoon, it felt a little funny to step into the modern dance studio again. Jackie Sanchez wasn't there to greet us—just my regular classmates warming up.

I didn't expect to be in the spotlight still, but as Luisa and I stretched, some of the other former pirate dancers peppered us with questions. What was Jackie like? What was she going to do with a smaller cast of pirates? Did she make us do any special exercises?

It was as if we were celebrities just because we had spent a few hours with Jackie. All the attention had been fun at first, but now it was getting annoying. Jade got that sort of treatment at school because everyone knew she was destined for great things. Did my sister ever get tired of it?

When Mr. Amici came into the studio, he cleared his throat noisily. "The last time I checked," he said, "this was a modern dance class, not a tea party."

We all hurried onto the floor to begin warming up as Mr. Amici walked around, making sure that we were stretching properly. He wore a turtleneck and loose yoga pants—all black, as usual. I wondered if he'd worn black when he was Jackie's teacher, too. Then I remembered the small crack in the mirror and had to bite my lip to keep from giggling.

Suddenly Mr. Amici's shadow stretched over

me. "I hope rehearsals went well on Saturday, girls," he said, looking at Luisa and me but speaking loudly enough for the whole class to hear. "You can learn a lot from Jackie, you know—not just about technique but also about what it takes to become a great dancer. I've never seen anyone work harder than she did when she was a student here. It was her work habits as well as her talent that made her a star. Keep that in mind, you two."

"Yes, sir," I said with a gulp.

He nodded and said, "Good." Then he pivoted and faced the rest of the class. "So today, I want all of you to dance like something that *floats*." He swept his arm in a wide arc. "And by the end of the dance, we should know exactly what you are."

One student puffed out his cheeks and danced like a balloon. Another was a kite. Luisa ran, twirled, and bounced all over the studio, and we finally guessed that she was a boat on a stormy sea.

As soon as Mr. Amici had announced the exercise, I thought of my sea fairy. When it was my turn to dance, I moved on all fours across the floor, arching my back and lowering and lifting my head like foam floating over rolling waves. Then I rose up like sea spray lifted by the wind. And I began to dance as I had last night with the moon.

I thought I'd done a good job being the sea fairy, but no one could guess what I was. And when I told them, Mr. Amici scratched his nose. "It was a good attempt, Isabelle," he said. "It just needs a bit more work."

I sank back down beside Luisa, trying to hide my disappointment. Being a sea fairy was a lot trickier than I'd thought it would be.

The next Saturday in the studio, I handed Jackie the sample cape. I held my breath as she lifted it up in front of a window. In the morning sunlight, the cloth glowed like pale emerald glass.

"Ooh, I love the design and the colors, Isabelle," she said. "It's wonderful!"

"It's fun to play with, too," Luisa said.

"Oh? Show me," Jackie said, handing her the cape.

Luisa took the cape and fastened it around her neck. As she began to spin, the cape rose around her.

"Yes, yes," Jackie said eagerly. "And then there's this, too. Grab the hem with both hands, Luisa." Jackie put her own fists below her waist. Then, turning her back on us, she extended her arms behind her and alternated swinging them up and down.

When Luisa tried that, her cape spread like butterfly wings. I suddenly realized that if lots of dancers did that at the same time, we'd form a solid wall of whirling, swirling green. "Maybe *all* nine of us could play with our capes at the same time during the show," I suggested.

Jackie's eyes gleamed as she pictured it. "Yes, the cast can do that during the entrance and exit," she agreed. "You really have a knack for this, Isabelle." Then she frowned. "But are you sure that you and your mother can make enough capes for everyone?"

I nodded eagerly. "I can cut the material for the capes, and my mom can hem them. But we'll need more material," I added. "May I text my mom and tell her?"

"Yes, please do," said Jackie.

So I pulled out my phone and sent off a quick text to Mom. But then I had another idea. "Maybe all the capes could have designs," I said to Jackie. "Jacob's and Saafi's could have crowns because they're doing Shakespeare. We could have a violin for Ryan and musical notes for Hailey. And flowers for the Waltz-ing Flowers, of course!"

Jackie stared at me. "You're a regular little fire-cracker, aren't you, Isabelle?" she said, breaking into a laugh. "But have you had time to think about your own character's costume yet?"

I hesitated. The sea fairy had seemed like such a good idea, but then I'd bombed in Mr. Amici's class when I'd tried to dance the part. "You said to think outside the box," I began nervously, "so . . . maybe I could be a sea fairy. And when I see Luisa dancing, I start to imitate her—sort of like the copycat game last week."

Jackie folded her arms. "Interesting," she said. "What's your costume going to look like?"

"I was thinking that I could wear an ivory leo-tard and tutu," I said, recalling Jade's postcard. "Like a sea fairy that's the same color as the whitecaps on the waves."

Jackie nodded. "I like it," she said, which made me tingle with relief. "It's good to make yourself look different from Luisa, whose costume will be very col-orful. And next week I can bring a simple prop or two that could help with your sea fairy routine."

"Really?" I asked.

"Absolutely. I know lots of stage tricks," Jackie said with a wink. "But for today, let's concentrate on learning your solos. Luisa, I'll demonstrate yours first."

I got goose bumps thinking that Jackie was going to dance for us. This was like having our own private performance!

She started the pirate music, nodding her head along with the first few notes. "We'll begin with a hornpipe move," she said, hopping on her right foot while bending and raising her other leg. Then she hopped on her left foot and lifted her right leg.

"Now, watch carefully," Jackie said, skipping sideways in one direction and then back toward where she started. "And then this." She skipped forward a step, and then skipped forward again with one leg bent and raised. She did another skip on the same foot and kicked the other leg upward. Then she reversed it all so that she wound up back in the same spot.

Some of the hornpipe steps looked familiar, but Jackie had added new arm movements, maybe because she had seen last week how flexible Luisa's shoulders and arms were. Jackie spread her arms to the sides, bending her elbows and pointing her hands downward. At the same time, she rolled her head around like a rag doll.

She swung her arms and kicked her legs as if she were just discovering them. And she seemed to love having them—maybe for all the ways they bent and wriggled. Her joyful movements became more and more smooth until she was gliding across the stage as gracefully as a butterfly.

I almost clapped when Jackie finished demonstrating, but I caught myself.

"Now we'll try it together one step at a time," Jackie said.

Luisa rose hesitantly, uncertainty clouding her face, but Jackie repeated the steps at a much slower tempo this time. Instead of playing music, she kept time with her hands, singing, "Da, DUM, da, DUM" while Luisa moved in slow motion. I tried the steps, too. I couldn't help myself! Every now and then, Jackie would adjust one of our arms or legs with a tap of her hand.

After Luisa had practiced the steps a few times, she looked relieved to realize that she could actually do the routine. When she tried it at full speed, she struggled with a few combinations, but Jackie didn't seem to mind demonstrating them for her again.

"Good," Jackie said approvingly as Luisa finished her routine.

"I made a lot of mistakes, though," Luisa said.

"But you've got the idea more or less," Jackie said. Then she turned to me. "And now, let's try your solo, Isabelle."

Jackie started out with a couple of hops on her right foot. Her other leg was raised slightly, the knee bent so that her left foot was behind her right leg. Then she reversed the move, hopping on her left foot with her right foot behind her.

Next, she did another pair of hops on each foot, but this time she kicked the opposite leg forward. Then she launched into a leap. My excitement grew as I saw how Jackie had tailored the routine for me— with the jumps that I liked to do. I couldn't wait to run through my solo! As I watched Jackie, my body began moving on its own, my arms and legs shifting slightly with each step.

On my first attempt at the solo, I did it in slow motion as Jackie kept time with her hands. About halfway through, though, I forgot the next step.

"Like this," Jackie said. Rising on her toes, she took quick, small steps across the floor, swinging her head from side to side with each step.

I watched myself in the mirror as I did my best to copy her.

When we had finished, Jackie gave me her notes. "When you land after a leap, I want you to put all your energy way up here," she said, tapping the base of my neck.

I tried a leap again and discovered that I stood a little straighter when I landed. I liked how my reflection looked in the mirror, so I made a mental note to try to remember that tip from now on.

After a few more repetitions, Luisa and I finally got to do our solos to music. And I began thinking about ways to visualize the steps so that I'd remember them. I pictured the sea fairy skipping over the waves. When I took a leap, I would rise like a spray of water hitting a rock.

When it was time to rehearse the ending of our routine, Jackie gave us another one of her tips. "You're going to feel tired by the time you get to this point," she told us. "But remember, you're the climax of the whole show. You've got to leave the audience feeling excited and joyful."

"So show lots of dance juice," I said, mostly to myself.

"What?" Jackie asked, giving a half laugh.

"My mom said I had a lot of it when I was little," I explained. "I was always dancing."

Jackie smiled. "Yes, dance juice—I like it," she said. "Do you know how I keep my dance juice flowing? I try to picture someone special in the audience—someone I'm performing especially for and wouldn't want to disappoint. Can you girls think of someone special you might picture?"

"My brother, Danny," Luisa said right away. Her brother was in the army, stationed in Texas, and I knew she missed him a lot.

"Good," said Jackie. "What about you, Isabelle? Is there someone special you can think of?"

"Sure, my sister," I said.

Jackie nodded. "Family's great," she said. "Okay, so let's practice the end of the routine."

As I followed her back out onto the floor, though, I couldn't help wondering, *Who is the special person you think of, Jackie?*

When I got home from rehearsal, a recording of Dad's "Pond Dreams" song floated through the house. He'd named it after Mom's mobile, and it was Jade's and my new favorite song.

"Hey, Isabelle!" Jade called from the living room. "I'm in here."

Costumes and Capes

I was eager to get into the sewing room to start making more capes, but when I poked my head into the living room, I was surprised to see that Jade had already unrolled the shimmery green material across the rug. The cardboard tube lay bare. Concentrating hard, with her tongue sticking out from a corner of her mouth, Jade was starting to cut out the first cape.

"What're you doing?" I asked. "Where's Mom?"

Jade's scissors went *snick-snick-snick*. "When she got your text, she went to pick up more fabric," Jade explained. "And I thought I'd give you a head start on the capes."

Jade sometimes helped us make costumes, but only when Mom or I asked her to. "Did Mom ask you to help?" I asked. "You don't have to, Jade. I know you're busy."

She grinned. "This was my idea," she said. "You're my little sister. I'm always there for you when you need me, right?"

"Right." I smiled. My big sister was coming to the rescue, as always.

I figured there was enough material for two more capes, so I went to get another pair of scissors from the sewing room. But as I passed by the bathroom, I heard scratching inside. "Oh, poor Tutu, did

53

you get locked in?" I asked.

"*M-rowrrrr,*" Tutu answered pitifully.

"Don't open the door!" Jade shouted from the living room. "I had to put Tutu in there while I cut the capes or she would have shredded them."

I could just picture Tutu pouncing on the capes, claws extended. "Sorry, Tutu," I said, taking my hand off the doorknob.

When I came back into the living room, Jade stood up to show me her work. "Well, that's one cape cut now," she announced proudly.

But I saw instantly that the cape was too long. It reached almost to the floor!

"Didn't Mom give you the measurements?" I asked, trying to control my wobbly voice. "The cape is only supposed to reach to the waist."

Jade shrugged. "I didn't decide to do this until after she left," she said.

Now I couldn't keep the frustration from my voice. "But you used too much fabric," I said. "What if Mom can't get more? We're going to get only *one* more cape out of it now instead of two!"

Jade stiffened. "Why are you shouting at me?" she asked. "I was just trying to help."

I took a deep breath. "Look, I appreciate it,"

I said, "but . . ." I didn't know how to tell her that she was making things harder rather than easier.

"I get it," Jade said. "This is what happens when I try to do something I'm not good at." She draped the cape across the coffee table and turned to leave the room.

Now I felt bad. "Forget I said anything," I said quickly. "Stay, Jade. Please?"

"No, I'll stick to ballet from now on," she said, not looking me in the eye. "I'll leave design to you."

Jade was just heading upstairs when Mom and Dad got home.

"We come bearing fabric and . . ." Dad boomed, holding up two white paper bags.

Jade and I instantly forgot about our fight. "Crab!" we both shouted. The scent was already making my mouth water.

"We stopped by the Fish Wharf on the way home," Dad explained. The Fish Wharf was actually a set of barges with shops floating on the Potomac River just a little ways from the Jefferson Memorial. "Maybe we should lock up Tutu before we eat," Dad added, looking around. "Last time we spent half the meal shoving her off our laps."

Tutu mewed from the bathroom, right on cue.

"Already done," I said, giggling. "Remember that time she got into the crab leftovers? She was such a mess, it took both Jade and me to clean her up." I glanced over at Jade, but she was opening one of the paper sacks and didn't look up. Was she still feeling bad about the cape?

We never bothered with plates or silverware when we had Fish Wharf crab. We would just set out four mallets. After spreading newspapers on the kitchen table, we would tear open the paper sacks so that there were two piles of crab. And then it was every girl for herself. Oh, and Dad, too.

Lunch was very noisy as we tapped at the claws with mallets. But I still managed to fill Mom and Dad in on practice. "Jackie liked my idea of designing capes for every dancer," I said proudly.

"If you have enough fabric for that," Jade sighed. So she *was* still thinking about her mistake.

"We have more than enough material now," Mom assured us. "In fact, I bought extra. Do you want to make a cape for Jackie, Isabelle?"

For Jackie? I hadn't even thought of that, but . . . "Yes, definitely!" I said.

Dad gave a low whistle. "That's a lot of capes," he acknowledged. "You two are going to be busy."

"I'm going to start right after lunch," I promised. "I want to do most of the work myself so that Mom doesn't have to."

Mom gave me a grateful smile, but later, as we started to clean up, she said she *wanted* to help me. I glanced at Jade, hoping she would offer to help again, too, but she was washing her hands at the sink, her back turned.

"And how is your own costume idea coming?" Mom asked me.

"I got Jackie's okay on it," I said. "I'm going to be a sea fairy, like the picture on Jade's postcard." I looked over at Jade. "Thanks for the idea, sis."

Jade shrugged. "At least I could help you with that," she said as she dried her hands.

I felt bad about hurting my sister's feelings, but once I was settled into Mom's sewing room, I started worrying about something else: the design for Jackie's cape. Figuring out designs for my castmates had been easy. Coming up with a design that would be worthy of Jackie Sanchez, though, would be the *real* challenge.

At the next rehearsal, Jackie greeted Luisa and me carrying a large bolt of blue material. Was this the special prop that Jackie had promised she'd bring for my sea fairy routine?

With a snap of her wrists, she sent the cloth unfurling across the studio floor like a sapphire carpet. "Luisa, take one end and walk toward that wall," she directed. "Isabelle, you take the other end and walk to the opposite wall."

When we were standing across the room from each other, Jackie told us to hold the cloth with both hands and wave it up and down. We tried it, and the cloth spread and billowed, as if alive.

"It's like the waves of the ocean," I said.

"Exactly! And I've got another bolt just like that," Jackie said. "Some of your castmates can be wave makers for your number." She motioned to Luisa. "You'll come onstage, Luisa, and begin your dance. And Isabelle . . ." Squatting down, she crept under the rising and falling cloth and then sprang back up. "You'll appear from out of the waves and be fascinated by Luisa. Once the wave makers leave the stage with the cloth, you'll begin to imitate Luisa."

Jackie took over holding my end of the cloth so that I could practice my entrance. It felt magical to spring up from beneath that blue band like a fairy from the sea.

I held on to that feeling while we practiced our solos and our closing routine. And at the end of rehearsal, when Jackie, Luisa, and I crossed our index fingers and whispered "shipmates," this time I felt as if we really were.

We'd no sooner lifted our hands away when a phone rang. Jackie hurried to her dance bag. "I've got to take this, girls," she said, waving an apologetic good-bye.

The school was silent as Luisa and I left the studio. I figured we must have been the last cast members to leave, but I wasn't complaining.

Outside, I took in a deep breath of fresh air. It was such a sunny spring afternoon that I didn't want to waste it. "You doing anything now?" I asked Luisa.

"Mom and I are going to bake some *sequilhos* to send to Danny," Luisa said. "They crumble in the mail, but at least that way, Danny doesn't have to share them with his buddies."

I giggled. I loved sequilhos, the melt-in-your-mouth cookies that Luisa's family makes from corn-starch, butter, and sweetened condensed milk.

Maybe Jade and I can bake some cookies this

afternoon, too, I thought to myself, reaching for my phone so that I could call her. After scolding her about the cape, I figured we were due for some sister time— if she wasn't practicing or studying.

I dug deep into my bag for my phone, but it wasn't there. Had it had fallen out in the studio?

"I can't find my phone," I said to Luisa. "I've got to go back to school before they lock the doors."

"Okay," Luisa said. "I'll save some sequilhos to bring to you on Monday—if Dad doesn't find them first."

"Thanks!" I said. But since Luisa's dad was as good at sniffing out treats as Tutu, I didn't have my hopes up.

I hurried back to school and up the steps. To my relief, one of the doors was open, and I ran along the hallway toward the modern dance studio. I started to push open the door to the studio but paused when I heard Jackie's voice from inside. She sounded frustrated.

"I'm just not free right now, Jean-Claude," Jackie said. "You'll have to find someone else to dance Odette."

Odette? Wow. Odette was a major role in *Swan Lake.* Was Jackie turning down that role?

I peeked through the crack of the door and saw that Jackie had her phone pressed to her ear. She was pacing back and forth, the rubber soles of her sneakers squeaking against the vinyl floor. "I know this kind of opportunity doesn't come along very often, but I still have to say no," she said again. "I'm sorry. I have important commitments."

I tried to close the door before Jackie could see or hear me, but the lock clicked loudly. I'd gotten just a few feet down the hall before the studio door opened and Jackie called, "Isabelle, is that you?"

"I'm sorry," I called back. "I didn't realize you were in the studio. I came back to look for my phone."

"Don't worry," she said, smiling. "I found it for you." She motioned for me to come back inside and then pulled my phone out of her bag. "So, you heard my conversation?" she asked.

"Part of it," I admitted, my cheeks flushing.

Jackie sighed. "The principal in New York City Ballet's *Swan Lake* injured her ankle during rehearsals, and they didn't think her understudy was ready," she explained. "Promise not to tell anyone that I turned them down?"

"I promise," I told her, although I wondered how I could keep news like this from Luisa or Jade.

Jackie arched an eyebrow. "That phone call left me feeling kind of restless," she said. "I need to work off some energy. Feel like dancing a little more?"

I hesitated. "You mean with *you*?" I asked.

Jackie smiled. "I think we're still warmed up, right?" she said. "I feel myself brimming over with dance juice."

Reaching into her bag, Jackie took out her phone, as well as a pair of pointe shoes. The ribbons dangled down over her hands. "Do you remember your flower routine from the Autumn Festival?" she asked me.

"I think so," I said as I reached into my bag for my own ballet slippers. Then I watched, fascinated, as Jackie wound the ribbons of her pointe shoes around her ankles and tied a knot, tucking the ends neatly under one of the bands. She did it so expertly and easily. How many thousands of times had she done this same thing?

She got to her feet and tapped first one foot on the floor and then the other, as if making sure her shoes were securely on her feet. Then she scrolled through the list of songs on her phone. "Ready?" she asked.

I got to my feet and stepped in position. "Yes,

ma'am," I said, swallowing hard. Who would believe I was going to dance with Jackie? It was so far beyond anything I had ever dreamed of.

As I heard the familiar notes of the French horn, Jackie suddenly rose *en pointe,* and I caught my breath. She started moving along the floor with a series of quick, soft taps of her shoes. From a distance, I knew it would seem as if she were gliding across the floor, but up close I could see how hard her leg muscles were working.

Jackie glanced over her shoulder and raised her eyebrows when she saw me standing like a statue— with my mouth open. She motioned for me to join her.

Don't just watch. This is the chance of a lifetime, I told myself. I pictured a water lily floating in the pond, my visualization for this dance, and began to move alongside Jackie.

It had been months since I'd danced the Waltzing Flowers routine, so there were moments when I struggled. But Jackie seemed to have eyes in the back of her head, and whenever I was having trouble, she turned to smile encouragingly. Then she would gesture gracefully or demonstrate a step so that all I had to do was follow her lead for a while.

I knew that Jackie could have performed this routine with much more complicated moves. The difference between her skill level and mine was like the distance between the moon and me. But she deliberately kept her moves simple so that I could follow along. She held back to let me feel like a true partner.

As I leapt into the air, Jackie rose beside me, dancing higher and farther and longer so that I really felt as if I were dancing with the moon. And as I leaped with Jackie again, my heart nearly burst with excitement and happiness. I wanted to put this moment into a glass globe so that I could keep it forever.

When we were done, we sat with our backs against the wall, trying to catch our breath. "It's been a long time since I danced just for the fun of it," Jackie said. "I have to do this more often."

"Don't you dance all the time?" I asked.

Jackie rolled her head against the wall to look at me. "Yes, but between ballet classes and learning choreography for performances with New York City Ballet, I never have time to dance just for myself," she said. "I was always doing that when I was small, especially with my abuelita—my grandmother. She was a folk dancer, and dancing was as natural for her as breathing." Jackie smiled as she remembered. "She'd dance in place when she cooked at the stove and then danced as she brought the bowls of food to the dinner table. Sometimes when the bowls were full, I'd follow her with a towel to mop up the spills."

I giggled. "I was always dancing, too, when I was little," I said. "I knocked over so much stuff that my parents had to keep all the breakables up high."

"Ah, so you were born a dancer as well," Jackie said, smiling. "When did you know you wanted to dance ballet?"

I didn't have to think before I answered. "When I saw my older sister's recital," I said.

Jackie nodded. "My grandmother took me to the HDC as a birthday present," she said. "I can only guess how many tables she waited on to buy the tickets. It was love at first sight for me. When I saw those ballerinas, I knew that's what I wanted to be. And once I started dancing, I couldn't stop. Abuelita called me *la mariposa*, which means 'the butterfly,' because I was always flitting around."

Butterfly? Funny, that's exactly how I had

thought of Jackie when I saw her demonstrating Luisa's solo a week ago.

Jackie thought for a moment and then said, "Ballet still makes me feel like nothing else, like I'm wet and cold and shivering in the rain and then"—she raised a hand in the air—"a ray of sunlight pokes through the clouds and pulls me up with it. I float upward on a breeze and leave everything else behind."

I finally worked up the nerve to ask the question that had been stewing inside me. "But if you love ballet so much, why did you turn down Odette?" I asked, glancing sideways at Jackie. "Why are you putting on these shows instead?"

"Because someone lifted me into that sunshine, and now it's time to give back," Jackie said simply. "Dancing isn't just about feeling joy, Isabelle. It's about spreading it around. It's a gift you are born with and a gift you can give to others."

Jackie suddenly reached for her bag. "Speaking of gifts," she said, "I have something for you. The school asked me for a memento for its trophy case, but I think you deserve these more."

Opening her dance bag, she took out a pair of girl's pointe shoes in a protective plastic bag. "This was my very first pair of pointe shoes," said Jackie. "They're too worn to use when you finally go en pointe, but maybe you'd like them as a souvenir?" She handed the shoes to me.

The toes were scuffed and the soles dark with wear, but those shoes might as well have been pure gold to me. Even so, I tried to give them back. "I can't take them," I said softly. "They're too special."

But Jackie insisted, pressing the shoes into my hands. "Take them, Isabelle, please," she said, "as a gift from one born dancer to another."

I couldn't speak over the lump in my throat, but as I held the shoes tenderly, I wondered what gift I could give to Jackie in return. *Just my best,* I thought. *I'll give her my best at rehearsals.* And then I remembered something else I could give her: a cape. A cape with a very special design on the back—the wings of a graceful butterfly.

When I got home, I heard clattering from the kitchen. I couldn't wait to tell Mom my news.

"I danced with Jackie!" I shouted happily. "Just her and me."

But it was Dad's voice that answered me. "You're kidding!" he said. "What was it like?" He was making hamburger patties, and Tutu was at his feet, waiting for something tasty to fall.

My mind was bursting with so many images and feelings that I didn't know where to begin. "Awesome" was all I could say. Then I remembered the shoes.

Unzipping my dance bag, I carefully took out Jackie's gift. "Look!" I announced, still in disbelief. "She even gave me her first pair of pointe shoes."

Dad dried his hands and studied the shoes from all angles, giving a low whistle of appreciation. "That's incredible," he said. "But they belong in something better than a bag." He stowed the hamburger patties safely inside the refrigerator and then said, "Follow me."

As he led me down the hall, Dad glanced over his shoulder and said, "Did you know my hospital signed up to host one of your shows?"

"That's great!" I said. It meant we could count

on at least one good audience. "We're also going to perform at Thompson Hospital," I added.

Dad sniffed. "I guess Thompson is an all-right place, if you're not *too* sick," he joked. Thompson was one of his hospital's friendly rivals.

Music floated out from the living room along with the rhythmic *thump* of feet. We stopped in the doorway. The furniture had been pushed against the walls to create a dance floor. Jade was moving through an intricate set of steps and looking as light as Mom's mobile whirling overhead. Her private lessons seemed to be worth every penny.

When Jade finished, she turned off the music on her laptop. "Do you like the new routine?" she asked, panting.

"It's amazing," I said.

"Beautiful, Jade. And Isabelle has something beautiful here to share, too," Dad said, stepping toward the fireplace mantel. I didn't understand what he was doing until he took down the cube-shaped glass case that held his boyhood treasure.

"That's your signed Cal Ripken baseball glove," I said.

"It won't turn to dust before I get another case," Dad said, setting the case down on the coffee table and lifting off the glass top. "It's just as important to protect Jackie Sanchez's shoes."

Jade whirled around and looked down at the shoes in my hands. "Are they really her pointe shoes?" she asked.

"Her first pair," I said proudly.

"Wow" was all Jade could say. Then she added, "You're getting really close to her, aren't you?"

I didn't want to brag, but I was feeling so proud that I had to share Jackie's compliment. "Jackie said she was giving them to me as a gift—from one born dancer to another," I said, feeling my cheeks burning.

"She did?" said Jade, cocking her head. *"Really?"* Jade narrowed her eyes, as if she thought I was making all of this up.

Jade's tone took the wind right out of my sails. Why was it hard for her to believe that Jackie would pay a compliment like that to me? Then it struck me: *Is Jade . . . jealous?*

Before I could respond, Dad asked, "Isabelle, do you want to do the honors?" He had removed his mitt from the display case, so it was ready for my treasure.

While I placed the shoes in the case, I noticed some words written inside one shoe. They were blurry from sweat and wear, so they were hard to read. "Wait, somebody wrote something," I said.

Dad crouched to study the words. "*Bue-na suer-te*," he read slowly. "That's Spanish for 'good luck.'"

As Dad gently lowered the glass case over the shoes, I wondered who had written the words. Was it Jackie's grandmother? If so, they were a doubly special gift. She was the one who had inspired Jackie's dancing and had taken her to her first ballet.

Then I wondered, *Is Jackie's grandmother her special person—the one she pictures in the audience to help lift her out of the rain and into the sunshine?*

At our last rehearsal before spring break, Luisa and I had polished our pirate routine, but we were still working on perfecting our stage entrance. Gabriel, Ryan, Jacob, and Hailey were the wave makers who rippled the blue cloth to create ocean waves. Jackie had added some surf sounds to the beginning of our music, and when Luisa heard the sound, she would dance out in front of the wave makers. Then I would creep beneath the layers of cloth and leap out, like a sea fairy springing from the frothy waves.

Now that there were two bolts of cloth
swirling around me, though, it was tougher to emerge
gracefully from the waves. I wished we could have
practiced our entrance for more than half an hour, but
our castmates had their own rehearsing to do.

Jackie spent the second half of the morning
working with the Waltzing Flowers. When their
rehearsal ended, I could hear Renata bragging from
way down the hall about the attention she was finally
getting from Jackie.

I was tempted to tell Renata about the pointe
shoes Jackie had given me, just to put her in her place.
But Renata might not be the only person who would
get jealous. My other castmates might, too, and that
wouldn't be good for the show. So I kept my mouth
shut, even though it was hard.

On the bus ride home, my stomach wouldn't
stop doing somersaults. Just two days from now, we
would be dancing for an actual audience!

As soon as I got home, I ran upstairs and
started to lay my costume out on my bed—and then
I realized I'd been so busy learning the pirate dance
that I hadn't even thought about my makeup. So
I went back downstairs to the living room, where Jade
was practicing.

The Pig-Hat Party

I knew enough not to interrupt her, so I just sat down in a corner out of the way. Her eyes drifted toward me, but she kept on dancing. When the song finally ended, she muted the sound on her laptop and turned toward me. "What's up?" she asked.

"We have our first show on Monday," I explained. "Would you do my makeup before I go?"

Usually my sister jumps right in to help, so I didn't expect her to shrug off my request. But she did. "Maybe it's time for you to start doing your own," Jade said.

What? She couldn't be serious. "But you're so good at it," I coaxed.

"You've seen me do it a lot of times, Isabelle," Jade insisted. "You can do it yourself—I know you can." She paused and then added, "Or Jackie can do it for you."

Jackie? "I can't ask *her*," I said, whining a little now. "She's too busy."

"And I'm not?" Jade snapped suddenly. "I've got my own lessons to worry about, you know." Wheeling around, she turned up the sound on her laptop, once again filling the room with music.

As my sister began to dance, I saw how stiff and tense she was. What had I said wrong? Was Jade really too busy to do my makeup, or was she just jealous of how close I'd gotten to Jackie?

I wish I knew how to make things okay between us, but I didn't have a clue. So I just left the room, feeling more alone than ever.

I was still feeling lonely and a little sad when I went to Anna Hart on Monday. Though school wasn't in session, we were using it as our gathering spot. A school bus was parked in the loading zone, and I saw some of the chaperoning parents gathered on the sidewalk.

Luisa and I changed into our costumes in the restroom. Luisa put on her pirate skirt with pink and orange flounces, and I put on my ivory leotard and tutu.

As usual, Renata hogged the mirror while she put on her makeup. No way was I going to ask *her* for help with mine. Lucky for me, though, just as Renata was leaving, Saafi came in to touch up her makeup. And when she was done, she agreed to help Luisa and me with ours.

Then, with Ms. Hawken and Jackie calling out instructions, we loaded up the bus and took our seats for the short drive out to Thompson Hospital.

Thompson was a tall slab of gleaming white concrete. When we walked through the sliding doors, I saw that the hospital was a lot newer than Dad's—with big windows that made it look lighter and airier inside.

But Renata frowned when she saw the visitors and staff streaming down the hallways. "It's as crowded as an airport in here," she said with a scowl.

"Yeah, hospitals are usually busy, Renata," I said, annoyed that she always had to complain about something.

We were all in costume, and each of us was carrying something. Luisa and I were lugging Dad's fun box full of costumes and props, while Gabriel was carrying the bag of capes.

Our chaperones and teachers doubled as pack mules, too. Ms. Hawken carried some sound equipment as we followed the hospital director down a wide corridor. The director was a small, round woman whose blouse had a bow at the neck the size of a sunflower. I wondered how she ate her lunch with that bow in the way.

"The cafeteria is the largest space for a show," she was explaining to Jackie. "It's not too busy after lunchtime, so we can move some of the tables aside."

The cafeteria turned out to be a large, low-ceilinged room. Janitors in blue uniforms had already folded up most of the tables and were pushing them toward one wall, their wheels squealing loudly.

Against the far wall gleamed the glass sneeze guards of the cafeteria line. Workers in white smocks and hairnets removed pans of food from steam tables. Other workers wheeled trolleys of trays and dirty dishes through swinging doors. From the kitchen came the *clang* and *clatter* of workers cleaning up.

"As you can see, the hot food service is finished," the director explained, "so you won't be in the way of the lunch crowd."

Luisa and I exchanged a glance. *Be in the way?* This woman made it sound as if she were doing *us* a favor, rather than vice versa.

Renata looked in disbelief at a large puddle of soup spilled on the floor tiles. "She's got to be joking," she muttered to Hailey. "How can anyone put on a show in here?"

"Shh," Hailey said. "She'll hear you."

But the director was still talking. "The children are scheduled to come down in an hour," she announced.

"The show's open to adults, too, though. Can you make a public announcement inviting anyone who is interested?" Jackie asked. She scribbled something on a slip of paper and handed it the director.

"Yes, of course," the woman assured her. "Now, I'll leave you to your setup." Turning on her heel, she hurried away.

Jackie motioned for us to gather around her. One corner of her mouth curved up. "Well, I warned you that this wouldn't feel like a theater," she said. "But we don't need a stage or fancy lights to entertain an audience. We just need ourselves and our talents." She motioned to the kitchen, which was as noisy as ever. "Even with all that going on, we're going to put on the best show we can, because what are we called?"

"Ah, the Big Hart Party?" Olivia asked timidly.

"That's right!" Jackie said, punching the air. "Let's hear it again."

This time we all said, "The Big Hart Party." And when Jackie cupped her hand behind her ear, we all shouted, "THE BIG HART PARTY!"

Satisfied, Jackie got down to business and marked off the area that would be our stage. We had no stage manager, so one of our chaperones, Olivia's father, was drafted into the job. He would keep the space clear while the audience gathered. And in the meantime, he got some paper towels from the kitchen and cleaned up the soup.

"Backstage" was marked off by folding screens that we'd brought from Anna Hart. They were solid wood planks with a gold-patterned satin covering. We dumped our props in the space behind the screens, which felt so empty compared with the crowded backstage areas at Anna Hart or the HDC's theater.

Next, Jackie got to work setting up the sound system. It was a pretty simple one: just two big speakers hooked up to an amplifier. A cable ran from that to an MP3 player, which Ms. Hawken would operate.

The only lighting was the steady glare from the fluorescent lights overhead. And there was no curtain, of course—just Gabriel to mark when one act ended and the next began.

We did a quick warm-up, and then Jackie asked Luisa and me to hand out the capes to the other dancers.

"Did you really have to put a parrot on mine?" Gabriel complained.

"If the cape fits, wear it," Luisa laughed.

When everyone had a cape, I cleared my throat loudly. "Excuse me, Jackie. We have a little something

for you, too," I said, my heart racing with nervous-
ness. I reached into my dance bag and carefully
pulled out a gold satin cape with a red butterfly
on the back.

"You made this for me?" Jackie said. "Oh, it's
beautiful, Isabelle!" As she reached for the cape, she
kissed my cheek.

Jackie knew how to do everything with style—
even putting on a cape. With a sweep of her arms, she
swirled the cloth outward and let it settle it around
her shoulders. Then she pirouetted, the cloth billowing around her, and we all started to applaud.

Jackie thanked us again, and then she put up
her hands to silence us. "Okay, Big Hart Party—let's
get started! When Ms. Hawken turns on the music,
we'll come through that door"—she pointed to a door
leading to a side corridor—"clapping our hands, like
we practiced at rehearsal. We'll keep clapping as we
form a row onstage and do our cape thing, and then
we'll march behind the screen one by one—and all to
thunderous applause," Jackie assured us with a wink.

We broke into small groups to run through our
routines. Gabriel stood off to the side, fanning out
cards and murmuring as he practiced his act.

Suddenly, a man's voice crackled over the loudspeaker. "Come one, come all," he said in a stiff, flat tone, as if he was having trouble reading the announcement. "The, um . . . Pig-Hat Party is about to begin in the cafeteria."

Pig-Hat Party? I wasn't sure whether to laugh or cry.

Renata put her hands on her hips indignantly. "Who's a pig?" she demanded.

Jackie stifled a giggle. "Well, I never got good marks for my handwriting," she admitted. "Next time I'll print out the announcement."

Then we all started to laugh, because that was the only thing we could do. *So will Jade when I tell her,* I thought, because this was just the sort of thing she and I crack up about. But I also wondered sadly, *Will she even want to hear about the show?*

Normally Jade was the one who calmed me down before a performance, when the butterflies were whirling around inside me, and afterward, too, when I needed to tell her what went right—and what went wrong. But things had been so weird between us lately. For today's performance, at least, I was all on my own.

As we waited in the side corridor with Jackie, listening for our musical cue, we heard the cafeteria fill with the sounds of our audience—the excited voices of children, the sound of their footsteps, and . . . *thumps* and *squeaks*?

I couldn't help peeking through the door. Both grown-up patients and kids were thudding along on crutches to reach the folding chairs that had been set up for them. Others were in wheelchairs with squeaky wheels.

Renata peeked through the doorway beside me, and as a teenager walked by in a hospital gown wheeling an IV bag on a stand behind him, I watched the color drain from Renata's face. The boy took a seat in the front row.

I'd visited the hospital with my dad lots of times, so I felt right at home here. But clearly Renata did not. "Are you okay, Renata?" I asked.

She scowled at me. "I just don't know why they have to sit so close to us," she said. "How are we supposed to have any room to dance?"

I bit my tongue and turned away without saying a word. It was time to put on a smile for our audience. Maybe Renata couldn't, but *I* could.

When everyone in the audience was settled,

Jackie nodded to Gabriel. "Gabe, go in and introduce us," she urged.

"Okay," Gabriel whispered. He closed his eyes for a moment, and when he opened them, it was as if he'd put in new batteries. He charged through the door. "Hey, it's party time!" he hollered. "Ready for some fun?"

There were a few weak yeses.

Gabriel went on determinedly. "Welcome to the Big Hart Party. Wel-come, wel-come, wel-come," he said, clapping his hands to each syllable. "We're so glad to be here with you. Now help me invite our talented performers onto the stage. Come on, everyone." Some of the audience began to clap along.

Jackie picked up the rhythm. "Let's go," she said with a smile, nodding toward the door.

Heads swiveled as we made our entrance, the faces in our audience looking excited and hopeful. Renata was just ahead of me in line, but she was moving slowly and giving the people in the audience a wide berth. What was wrong with her? Was she afraid of catching something? That would be so like Renata—only worrying about herself. I nudged her from behind to keep going.

Once we had lined up in the space that was our

stage, the music began and we started to dance. The special part came when we pivoted and our capes billowed up around us, forming a green kaleidoscope of constantly changing shapes.

After our grand entrance, the cast began to pass out the hats, costumes, and props in Dad's fun box. The only one not helping was Renata—maybe because she was still worried about catching something. *Too bad she can't "catch" some good manners,* I thought sourly, but then I forced myself to smile. *Don't let her ruin this.*

As I handed a paper crown to a little five- or six-year-old boy, I saw the flash of disappointment on his face. "Would you rather have a different one?" I asked. "What's your favorite color?"

He looked up at me with bright blue eyes. "I wanted a pig hat," he said in a tiny voice.

"Oh, I'm sorry!" I said, smothering a smile. "That was a mistake in the announcement. But"— I looked around for someone with a marker—"maybe I can draw a pig on your crown."

Fortunately, a nearby nurse had a marker. I set the crown on an empty chair and carefully drew a picture of a smiling pig. "There you go," I announced. "One special pig hat."

When I set it on the boy's head, his smile lit up the room. Renata didn't know what she was missing.

We hurried back behind the screens and shed our capes, listening to Gabriel do a couple of card tricks. He was so good with the audience! Soon he had everyone laughing and clapping.

When Gabriel introduced "The Waltz of the Flowers," though, the kitchen grew noisier. *Bong! Bong! Bong!* It sounded as if the staff were hammering pots out of metal rather than cleaning them.

Olivia and Renata might as well have been trying to dance in a bell tower. When I peeked around the screen, I saw Renata stumble.

She was in tears by the end of her routine. "This is crazy," she muttered to me backstage. "How can anyone dance with all this noise?"

I'd like to say that things went smoothly after that, but they didn't. The props for Jacob and Saafi's act had just been dumped together in a box for the drive here, so it took a while to sort them out and put everything in its proper place onstage. Gabriel covered the delay with more card tricks and jokes— a lot better than the ones in Dad's book.

Even so, a bad case of nerves spread through the rest of the cast. Even when the kitchen grew quiet again, everyone looked discouraged.

We all knew we were giving only a so-so performance, but I didn't know how to turn things around. Jackie had invited me to be on the tour partly because she had seen me help a little dancer get over her stage fright before *The Nutcracker.* Maybe she thought that I could keep all of my castmates calm and on track, but today I sure was doing a crummy job of that.

When it was time for the pirate dance, I tried to focus on doing my very best dancing. So what if I had no theater or stage? No one had taken away my dance skills, and they had been good enough at the Autumn Festival and *The Nutcracker* to make people happy. I'd just have to rely on them here, too.

"To the stars?" I whispered the school motto to Luisa.

"To the stars," she said, nodding.

Jackie had wanted Luisa and me to be the fireworks at the end of the show. "We need *lots* of dance juice. Think of Danny out there," I said as I began to bob up and down on the balls of my feet to loosen up.

"And you think of Jade," Luisa said, hopping up and down beside me. But today, the thought of Jade made me more sad than safe. I shrugged off the feeling and lifted my chin, waiting for our cue.

The wave makers went out with the cloth ocean, and as the recorded sounds of surf washed over our ears, I saw Luisa's lips moving—counting the moments before she made her move. Just before the music began, she slipped around the screen and began dancing.

Crouching low, I followed her and scurried under the billowing cloth. As it rose and fell overhead, I felt as if I really *were* beneath the surface of a sea.

When I stood up at my cue, though, I'd mis-judged the distance. Instead of bobbing up between the two lengths of cloth, I stood up *underneath* one of them. The cloth bulged as I pushed against it. Hailey lost her grip, and her end of the ocean fluttered to the stage.

The audience started to laugh as I pulled the cloth away from my head. I wished the audience were laughing with us instead of at us, but at least it was a start. Only how do you make people feel joy when you don't feel joyful yourself?

I stretched my cheek muscles to pull up the corners of my mouth, but it was more of a scowl than a smile. And I felt like a robot going through pro-grammed motions, not a dancer. So much for making anyone feel happy. I couldn't even do it for myself.

Our big finale with the capes didn't go much better. The cast swirled and clapped their hands with the audience, but nobody's heart was in it. We all seemed glad when the performance was finally over.

As the audience was leaving the cafeteria, we gathered up the hats and other props and put them back into Dad's fun box. Then Jackie rounded us up for a pep talk. "You did very well in a difficult situation," she said. "Every place we perform is going to be different, and so are the problems. You just have to learn to shake them off and go on."

That was the advice she had given me that had gotten me through *The Nutcracker,* so I knew it worked. But I think I was the only one here who believed her.

My dance bag felt as heavy as a bag of rocks as I trudged up the steps to our house. I felt as if I'd let Jackie down big-time. Not only had my dancing lacked joy, but I hadn't kept any of my castmates from getting nervous—including myself.

I just wanted to go to bed, pull the covers over my head, and not come out for a week. But when I opened our front door, I heard a steady *thwack-thwack-thwack* from the living room. That sound meant Jade was working on a new pair of ballet shoes.

Pointe shoes have a kind of stiff box inside the toe to support a dancer's weight. The boxlike part of new shoes has to be softened before a dancer can wear them.

I dropped my dance bag in the hallway and scooped up Tutu. Cradling her in my arms, I hesitated in the hallway by the living room, wondering if I should go inside. Would Jade feel like talking with me? Was she too busy?

Finally, I made up my mind to step into the room. I was feeling awful, and I knew that Jade was the only one who could make me feel better.

Jade was sitting with her legs spread as she hit her shoe against the floor. She glanced up at me and then back down at her shoes, not saying anything at first. But after a moment she asked, "How was the show?"

I didn't even know where to start. I was afraid if I opened my mouth, I'd just start crying. I plopped onto the sofa and began scratching Tutu under her chin.

Jade took one look at my face and lowered the shoe. "What's wrong?"

I took a deep breath and shook my head, discouraged. *"Everything,"* I was finally able to say. "We were in this awful cafeteria, with no room to move. And the kitchen was so noisy that it threw everyone off. And . . ." I thought for a moment, trying to figure out what the worst part had been. Then it hit me. "And *you* weren't there, Jade. When everything bad was happening, I really needed to talk to you."

Jade's face softened. Then she said with a half smile, "That's funny, Isabelle, because I was pretty sure you didn't need me for much of anything anymore."

"What?" I said, sitting up. "Why would you say that?"

Jade shrugged. "Ever since you started dancing with Jackie, it's been 'Jackie this' and 'Jackie that.' She gave you tips about dancing that I never knew. And if you don't need me to help with your dancing, then what *do* you need me for?" Jade laughed halfheartedly as she added, "Definitely not for help with your capes or your costumes."

I couldn't believe I was hearing this from Jade. I mean, I'd suspected that she was a little jealous of my time with Jackie, but how could she ever think I didn't need her anymore? I didn't know whether to hug her or get down on the floor and shake some sense into her.

"Jade!" I exclaimed. "Of course I need you. I'll *always* need you. You're my person."

Jade gave me a questioning look. "Your person?"

"Yeah, you know how at the start of a show when you're nervous—or at the end of a show when you're starting to get tired—and you need something that makes you feel better?" I said.

Jade nodded slowly.

"Well, Jackie says . . ."—as soon as I said the name "Jackie," I saw Jade's face fall, but I went on quickly—"she says that I should picture someone special, someone who supports me and gives me energy. And I think of *you*, Jade. I always think of you."

Jade was silent then for such a long time. But when she came to sit beside me, I could tell by the look on her face that we were going to be okay. "That makes me feel good, Isabelle," she said, and then she leaned in and said the magic words: "And you know what might make us both feel even better? *Ice cream.*"

I laughed out loud. "Before dinner?" I asked.

"Before dinner," said Jade, grinning. "Mom

will understand." She threw her arm around me and squeezed me close.

I leaned my head on Jade's shoulder. I'd really, really missed her.

Then I remembered we had a show to do again tomorrow, and I sat up straight. "Jade," I said, "there's something I need even more than ice cream."

Jade sat up, too. "No way," she said, mocking me.

"No, really," I said, turning to face her. "I have another show tomorrow, and . . . well . . . would you do my makeup?"

Jade smiled. She nodded her head slowly. "You got it, sis," she said softly.

I smiled, too, and gave Jade another hug. I had my sister back, and suddenly tomorrow looked a whole lot brighter.

The next morning, as we gathered by the bus at school, my castmates tried to act cheerful, but I could tell they were pretending. They laughed too loud and too quickly, their smiles flashing on and off like lamps short-circuiting.

As for me? I was determined to do my job today—to spread joy with my dancing and to help my castmates feel less nervous. But after a few minutes with Jackie, my determination faded. She seemed strangely quiet. After sacrificing so much to organize the tour, including turning down the role of Odette in *Swan Lake*, I wondered if she was sorry she'd done it. Was it too late for me to help turn things around?

When we boarded the bus, I sat down beside Luisa. Renata was sitting in front of us, and she turned around and looked pointedly at me as she said, "It's important that you don't mess up today."

"Hey," Luisa said indignantly, "you made plenty of mistakes yourself, Renata."

I put a hand on Luisa's wrist to stop her before she said anything else. "I know we're all going to try our best," I said.

"You can't just *try*. You've got to *be* your best," Renata insisted. "My parents and brother, Ben, are coming to see us today."

"Really?" I said with genuine interest. I'd never seen Renata's family at a performance before, and I was surprised they'd come to an "on the road" show like this one. "That's great," I started to say, but Renata had already turned back around.

When we reached the grounds of the nursing home, Gabriel let out a whistle and said, "Fancy."

"Very fancy," Renata agreed, gazing out the window at the ten-story brick building built in a U shape around a fountain. "It must cost a fortune to stay here." She was always talking about how much things cost, especially the expensive ballet costumes her family bought for her.

The director, a small man with wire-rimmed glasses and a fringe of hair around his bald head, met us out front. "We're honored to have you, Ms. Sanchez," he said, reaching for her hand.

"Thank you," Jackie said, and then she whispered something to him.

"Yes, of course," the director said, nodding.

Jackie turned to us. "You'll have to excuse me for a little while, kids," she said. "Someone from the home will show you where to set up, and

Ms. Hawken will supervise."

"I'll send my secretary, Ms. Perl, to take care of you," the director told us over his shoulder. And the next moment, he and Jackie disappeared inside. Where were they going? How were we going to set things up without Jackie? Beside me, Luisa looked just as worried as I felt.

Ms. Hawken didn't waste any time, though, putting us to work. We were unloading the bus when a pleasant, gray-haired woman came out of the home. "I'm Ms. Perl," she said, introducing herself to Ms. Hawken. "Would you kindly follow me?"

Each of us picked up something to carry and followed her into the lobby. Giant tapestries with colorful abstract designs hung on the wood-paneled walls. This looked like the lobby of an expensive hotel. Renata was beaming with approval.

In one corner, a few plush couches had been arranged around a large-screen television. A dozen elderly people sat watching a soap opera, with the volume turned way up. Most of them wore everyday clothes. But one woman had dressed up in a formal blue dress and pearl necklace, as if she were dining at a fancy restaurant. She turned to look at us excitedly.

A place as ritzy as this might even have its own

theater and stage, I thought. So I was surprised when Ms. Perl led us to another narrow sitting area just beyond the information desk. "We thought this would be the most suitable spot," she said.

I looked around at the staff, visitors, and nursing home residents passing through the area. This spot was so public that we might as well be performing out on the sidewalk. And we would be competing with the noise from the TV. As I glanced backward, a man in a green cardigan turned up the volume even louder.

Where is Jackie? I wondered. *We need her!*

After Ms. Perl excused herself, Ms. Hawken clapped her hands to get our attention. "Okay, let's start setting up," she said.

Renata looked around sourly. "Why bother, Ms. Hawken?" she asked. "This 'stage' is the size of a postage stamp. This is going to be a disaster, just like yesterday."

I could tell from the way everyone else's shoulders were slumping that they felt the same way. But I wasn't going to stand by and let things fall apart this time. "So what if this isn't the best spot?" I said brightly. "If I weren't dancing here today, I'd probably be dancing at home in my living room—which is a lot smaller than this." I turned to Hailey. "What about you, Hailey?"

Hailey smiled and tucked her brown hair behind one ear. "I guess I'd be practicing my singing," she agreed.

"Sure," Luisa chimed in. "Think about this as the dress rehearsal we never had." I could always count on my friend to back me up.

Gabriel pointed to an area on one side of the room. "Ms. Hawken, look at those curtains," he said. "Don't they look like theater curtains?"

The wine-colored velvet curtains hung from tall windows and had gold cords pulling them away from the glass panes. When Ms. Hawken unhooked the cords, the curtains swept down in front of the windows, making the perfect backdrop for our per-formance. "Let's place our 'backstage' screens beside them," Ms. Hawken said, sounding pleased.

When we were done setting up, the rich win-dow curtains and fancy screens really *did* look like the backdrop of a theater. The stage space, though, was a lot smaller than we were used to. Luisa and I prac-ticed some dance moves to see how far we could travel across the floor. As we danced, I noticed the well-dressed woman watching us from across the lobby.

A Very Special Guest

"I hope I remember everything," Luisa sighed when we were done.

"I hope Jackie shows up soon," I said, scanning the hallway.

But when the start time for our show came and went, there was still no sign of Jackie. People passing by looked at our stage setup curiously but didn't stop. When was Jackie going to come back and tell us to start? And how were we going to find an audience then?

Finally, Ms. Hawken couldn't take it anymore. "I'm going to look for Jackie," she said, hurrying away.

We stared at one another. Even the parent chaperones whispered nervously. Renata kept looking at her phone. Was her family running late?

I started getting just as discouraged as my cast-mates, but then I remembered the advice that Jackie had given me at *The Nutcracker*: "Things are going to happen that you can't control. You can't let it bother you. You have to try your best."

Remembering Jackie's words made me feel better. After all, we couldn't control whether we had an audience, right? Or . . . *could* we?

From all the times my dad's band had played at fairs and markets, I knew it was hard to gather an audience at the start of a show. But I also knew that all it took was one person—that if the band started to play for just one person, others would hear the music and come.

Maybe that would work here, too. I glanced toward the TV area. Then I took a deep breath and motioned to Luisa to follow me.

"Excuse me," I said loudly enough so that I would be heard over the TV. "We're from the Anna Hart School of the Arts, and we've come here to put on a show. We call it the Big Hart Party. Would any of you like to join us?"

Some of the residents didn't seem to hear me, but the woman in the blue dress smiled and rose stiffly from the sofa. "I was hoping you would begin soon," she said. She reached for the walker beside her.

As we made our way slowly back toward our stage area—with Luisa on one side of the woman and me on the other—she said, "You know, dear, I used to have season tickets to the Hart Dance Company."

"Really?" I said, surprised. "Wow, you must have loved ballet."

"Oh, I still do," said the woman. She patted her walker and said, "It's just too difficult to go now." She sighed and said, "My name is Ruth, by the way."

A Very Special Guest

Luisa and I introduced ourselves, and then we helped Ruth get settled in a chair in the front row. After we left her there and ducked around the screens, Luisa and I exchanged a smile. It felt good to know we were bringing our show to people like Ruth, who loved the ballet as much as we did.

Backstage, we found Gabriel warming up by flexing his fingers. I'd seen him do it lots of times, but I still found it hard to believe that a human being could bend his hands that way.

"Gabe," I said, "maybe you should start your act."

He hesitated. "Don't you think we should wait for Ms. Hawken or Jackie?" he asked.

"We have someone in the audience waiting for us to get started," I said. "A very special guest."

Gabriel nodded. He took a deep breath, transforming himself into the master of ceremonies. Then he bounced from around the screen and began to perform his tricks for Ruth. I felt a wave of relief when I heard her laughing.

When I peeked out from behind the screen, I saw that some of the other nursing-home residents had begun to drift over and sit down, too. Only the man in the green cardigan stayed stubbornly by the TV screen.

As the seats filled, my heart swelled. For once I'd solved a problem by myself, without Jade or even Jackie leading the way. Now I knew how a circus acrobat felt the first time she did her trapeze act without a net! Scared, but proud.

My other castmates seemed happy, too, but not Renata, who hung back alone by the wall.

"Isn't your family coming?" I whispered to her.

Renata shook her head. "They texted to say that a recruiter was coming to the house to talk to my brother." The rest of her words came out in a rush. "Ben's a big football star on his high school team. I guess his football stuff was more important than seeing me dance, as usual. My parents would do *anything* for him, but they treat me like I'm invisible."

I didn't know what to say. Renata had just shared more with me about her family than I'd ever heard before. I couldn't believe her family had ditched her performance, but *part* of what she'd said made sense to me.

"Do you . . . feel like you're in Ben's shadow sometimes?" I asked, choosing my words carefully.

She shook her head bitterly. "What would you know about it?" she snapped.

"*You* try being Jade's little sister," I said.

Renata's face softened. "Well, maybe you do know something after all," she admitted.

"It's hard," I said, "but I'm learning to stop comparing myself to Jade. Instead, I try to be myself, to focus on what *I'm* good at." I hesitated and then said, "And I know this much about you, Renata. You're a first-rate dancer."

"You don't mean that," she said, looking away.

"Jackie invited you to be in her show," I said, catching her eye again. "That's all the proof I need."

Renata pushed away from the wall and gave me the smallest hint of a smile. "Some days, Isabelle, you're not that much of a pain," she said.

I grinned at her, and during the silence that followed, I heard Gabriel still talking in front of the screen. "How's Gabe doing?" I asked Luisa, who was peeking around the screen.

She smiled nervously. "Well, the audience is still paying attention," she reported. "But, Isabelle, what if Jackie doesn't come back soon?"

Luisa was looking at me as if I were in charge of this production and had all the answers. In fact, *everyone* behind the screen was looking at me, waiting for the next cue. I thought for a moment and then said, "It's going to be noisy again with the television going, but we can't let it bother us. We have to block it out and do our best."

Some of my castmates nodded.

Just as I was about to tell Gabriel it was time to start, I heard the *ding* of elevator doors opening. I peeked around the screen and felt a rush of relief when I saw Jackie pushing a wheelchair out of the elevator. With her was Ms. Hawken, and in the chair was an elderly woman with the sweetest smile I'd ever seen.

Jackie wheeled the chair next to Ruth and then said, "Will all the cast come out, please?"

When we filed out in our capes, Jackie nodded. "I'm glad you carried on without us," she said. "That's a nice show of initiative."

"Thanks to Isabelle," Hailey murmured.

Jackie gave me a grateful smile. "I'm sorry that I wasn't with you during setup," she said, "but I had to check on my abuelita."

Her grandmother? Was this the special person Jackie had told me about—the one who had inspired her by taking her to her first ballet? I couldn't believe I was going to actually meet Jackie's grandma, let alone perform for her. I tingled with excitement.

Jackie put her hand on the elderly woman's

shoulder and said, "My grandmother had a health scare this morning, but fortunately it was a false alarm, and she's okay."

Suddenly I understood. *That's* why Jackie was so quiet before the show! She was worrying about her grandmother, not regretting setting up the tour.

Taking her grandmother's hand, Jackie turned to face the audience. "Abuelita worked extra jobs so I could take ballet lessons," she said, her voice thick with emotion. "She bought me my first pair of pointe shoes, and she has always been my biggest fan. I still call her before performances just so that I can hear her wish me *buena suerte*—good luck."

So Jackie's grandmother *had* written those words in the pointe shoes Jackie had given me. I was so busy thinking about the shoes that I almost didn't hear Jackie say, "Isabelle, will you get my cape?"

I slipped behind the screens and got the cape. When I delivered it to Jackie, she spread it out so that her grandmother could see the butterfly on it. "See what they made me?" she asked.

"*La mariposa*," her grandmother said, tracing the butterfly design with a trembling finger. "Yes, that's you."

"But I want *you* to wear this today," Jackie said as she draped it around her grandmother's shoulders. "Without you, I'd never have gotten to where I am. You gave me wings. So I want to dedicate today to you. Thank you for everything, Abuelita." She kissed her grandmother's cheek.

A hush fell over my castmates, maybe because we suddenly realized how important our performance today would be. We were performing for the person who had inspired Jackie Sanchez. We had to do well—for Jackie and for her abuelita.

Jackie's grandmother raised a frail hand to her mouth and called out to us in Spanish, *"A las estrellas."* Then she translated. "To the stars." Our school motto!

"Ms. Hawken," Jackie called, "will you start the intro?"

As the music began, I did my best to shut out the TV and concentrate on our performance. We *all* seemed to be trying our very best.

It wasn't until halfway through the show that I realized I couldn't even hear the TV anymore. When I peeked around the screens, I saw that the man in the green cardigan had turned off the television and was watching our show—and smiling!

A Very Special Guest

Jackie had been right yesterday. It didn't take a fancy stage or lights to make people happy. It took performers like us—people who were willing to take risks and overcome a few obstacles to perform for new audiences and to try to make them feel good. With our talents and our joy, we could transform a lobby or living room or lawn into a magical place of music, song, dance, and laughter.

And because that power was inside us, we could work that magic *anywhere*.

When it was time for me to dance, I was so nervous that I felt as if there were ants crawling up and down my spine. To calm down, I pictured Jade's face in the audience. Then I crept beneath the blue cloths that my castmates were waving, and energy surged through me. As the fabric rose and fell above me, I felt like a fairy looking up at an invisible moon that called, *Dance with me!*

It was a voice I couldn't resist. Heart beating, I leaped out of the waves like a dolphin. *Yes!* This time it was a clean jump between the two sections of cloth, and I stood beside Luisa.

What was this wonderful sound that filled my ears? And who was this colorful creature beside me, having such fun moving her arms and legs in those

amazing ways? I had to try it, too, and when I did, it felt so good that I couldn't stop smiling.

When it was time for my solo, I remembered the afternoon when I was dancing alone with Jackie. Happiness filled me again until I felt as weightless as a butterfly. With each step of my routine, I felt lighter and happier.

When the music finished, Ruth led the applause. Luisa and I ran behind the screens to get ready for the finale. Gabriel was holding out our capes, and as we draped them around our shoulders, I felt someone's hands helping to fasten the Velcro around my neck. I turned and saw Renata there, smiling at me.

She looked happy, even though she'd just performed on a tiny stage with a TV blaring in the background, even though the audience had been small— and her family wasn't in it.

So I gave Renata a big smile back and a quick hug before we all rounded the screens for our finale.

When we spread our capes, I felt like a butterfly spreading her wings. And as tired as I must have been, I knew I could have gone on dancing for hours.

I was a little sad when we met at school before our final show. Jackie must have been thinking the same thing, because as the others began to load the bus, she pulled me aside. "I really *felt* your joy yesterday, Isabelle," she said. "Everyone did. And with Ms. Hawken and me gone, you stepped right in and kept everyone focused and moving forward."

"I hope that was okay," I said.

"It's more than okay," Jackie said with a smile. "You've got so many skills. Not only are you a dancer, but you're a designer, too. And yesterday, you showed that you're also a leader. That means that someday you could be a wonderful teacher, or choreographer, or even director. So keep growing and developing your talents, okay?"

I nodded solemnly. Turning to walk back toward the others, I felt as if I were walking a foot above the sidewalk. Jackie made me feel like I could do *anything*. How'd she do that? I wondered if I could learn how to make others feel that way someday, too.

Dad's hospital was older than Thompson or the nursing home. As our bus pulled up in front of the brick building, I hoped Renata wouldn't make fun of it. But when I glanced at her, she was gazing out the window with a smile on her face. Was she anticipating our show? She had actually been acting pretty decent since our heart-to-heart talk yesterday.

Dad began waving both arms over his head as soon as he saw us. With him was Gabriel's sister, Zama, who was wearing the light blue smock of volunteer. My mom and Luisa's dad, Uncle Davi, had both taken the day off from work, so they were standing beside Dad, too. And so was *Jade*. Today, if I got tired or nervous during the show, I wouldn't have to just imagine her sitting in the front row. I could look out at the audience, and she'd be right there.

"Welcome, welcome," Dad started to shout, until Mom pointed toward the sign at the entrance: "HOSPITAL ZONE. QUIET PLEASE."

With Dad and Zama as guides, the show setup was a breeze. We rode the freight elevator up with our gear to the children's ward on the third floor. "At first, we were going to have you perform right here in the ward," Dad explained to Jackie. "But there's been such a demand, we had to move the show out into the sitting area."

He led the way to a large waiting area that was normally filled with couches, tables, and toys for children to play with. But today all of that had been replaced by folding chairs.

Jackie and Ms. Hawken quickly worked out where our stage would be, and the rest of us pitched in to set things up. We were finally getting good at creating our traveling theater. Too bad the tour was almost over.

We had just finished warming up when a woman in a purple coat took a seat in the front row. Next to her, in a wheelchair, was a little girl of about five with black hair, large eyes, and a smile that could have lit up all of Washington. She was taking in everything excitedly, just as Ruth had yesterday. That's when I noticed the heavy brace on her leg.

I suddenly felt lucky, and a little guilty. *Not only can you walk, but you can dance, too,* I told myself. *Don't ever take that for granted.* And I sprang forward into a practice leap.

When the little girl started to clap, I felt almost embarrassed. "Thanks," I said, waving at her.

The woman introduced herself. "I'm Didi Tyler, and this is my daughter, Trisha." She looked down at her daughter. "She's here to have an operation that will help her walk."

I stepped toward them. "Well, you've come to a

great place for that," I said, giving Trisha a reassuring smile.

The little girl said something to me in a shy, quiet voice.

"Could you repeat that?" I asked, bending over so that she could whisper in my ear.

Trisha leaned forward and said, "I want to be a dancer—like you."

I felt a lump form in my throat. I knew from other patients I'd met before that Trisha wasn't going to have it easy. Even after the operation, she might need months of therapy just to learn to walk, let alone dance.

But I wanted to encourage this little girl just as Jackie had encouraged me. So I smiled my warmest smile and nodded at Trisha. "Maybe someday I'll be watching *you* onstage," I said to her.

Trisha's face lit up as she sat back in her chair. I could see how much determination was packed into her little body. I had a feeling she *would* dance one day.

But today, I vowed silently, *I'll dance for you. I'll be your legs.*

I left Trisha there in the front row and ducked behind the screens, ready to put on the show of my life.

Mr. Kosloff, the director of *The Nutcracker*, had warned me that I had to ignore distractions while I danced, and Jackie had once told me I had to forget my mistakes. Now, after a week of performing on the road, I knew I could handle almost anything that came up. My castmates seemed to feel the same way. When the music echoed off the low ceiling today, we just smiled and carried on.

As we began to twirl and our capes billowed in the opening number, I saw Trisha clapping with delight. I caught sight of my family, too, and smiled at them. Since they had helped me create the capes, Trisha's applause was for them, too.

Jackie had said that she wouldn't be where she was today without her grandmother. And I knew that I wouldn't be dancing today either without Mom and Dad—and especially not without my big sister, Jade— cheering me along every step of the way. No matter where we were, Jade would always be with me, just as Jackie's grandmother would always be with her.

Now, here was Trisha. Was she watching me today the way I had watched Jade at her first ballet recital? Could I inspire Trisha the way Jade had inspired me? I was sure going to try.

I wondered if there was something special for Trisha in the fun box. When it was time to carry the box onstage, I felt someone right on my heels. I turned and was surprised to see *Renata,* reaching for the other handle of the box. She grinned at me as we carried it around the screen.

After we'd set the box down, Renata grabbed something out of it and made a beeline toward a well-dressed couple and a tall blond boy. Was this her family? As she plopped a goofy hat on the boy's head, his smile looked just like hers.

I dug in the box for something special for Trisha and found a headband with little gold stars on long, bouncy wires. Perfect! I helped her put it on, and she wagged her head back and forth so that the stars danced around her.

The party feeling carried over into the performances, too. When it was my turn to come out as a sea fairy, I'd never felt lighter or happier—my body warmed by that ray of sunlight Jackie had told me about.

As I leapt out of the cloth waves, I glanced at Trisha from the corner of my eye. She was leaning forward in her wheelchair, looking as if she was having the time of her life.

Well, so was I. I flashed her a big smile.

When I began to copy Luisa's moves in the opening of our act, I told myself, *More energy for Trisha*. Later, as I rose into the air in my first jeté, I said to myself, *Stronger, higher for Trisha!*

The expression on the girl's face was enough to make me leap even higher the next time—higher than the tallest ocean wave, so high that I could wrap my arms around the moon and bring it back for her.

It's funny, but as I danced, my heart grew lighter and yet fuller all at the same time. When our routine ended and it was time to put on our capes, I still felt strong and energetic.

Luisa and I were the last to file onstage, clapping and swaying to the music in our emerald green capes. We wound up at the end of the line, right next to Gabriel. Suddenly he stepped backward and beckoned to me. "You've got a fan," he said, smiling.

And then other castmates were backing up and pulling me toward the center. It was either move forward or fall on my face.

Renata was right in my path, but she smiled, too, and stepped aside to make room for me. And then I was standing right in front of Trisha. She was bouncing up and down in her wheelchair as she applauded. The look on her face was better than a stage full of bouquets.

Yes, I thought to myself, *I want everyone to feel like this: Trisha, Ruth, Jackie's grandmother, my parents, and Jade—like we could dance across oceans, like we could hug the moon.*

Letter from American Girl

Dear Readers,

When Isabelle joins a group of traveling performers that visits nursing homes and hospitals, she realizes how good it feels to tap into her talents to bring joy to others.

Here are the stories of some real girls who have used their passion for dance to help others. Meet Amiya, who teaches dance from a studio on wheels; stepsisters Izzy and Madi, who dance to raise money for charity; Drew, who raised money to buy ballet slippers for the homeless; and Grace, who makes tutus to raise money for sick children.

As you read these stories, think about the ways you might use your own talents to spread joy, too.

Your friends at American Girl

A Dance Studio on Wheels

Nothing in 11-year-old Amiya A.'s life has given her more joy than dancing, so she came up with an idea for how to share her passion with kids who couldn't afford dance lessons. Her plan? Get a school bus, paint it pink, replace the seats with dance barres, and hit the road with a mobile studio. She sketched plans for the bus on a piece of paper and talked about it with her mom.

Amiya wasn't sure her plan would work. "But if you have a dream and you work hard, your dream just might come true," she says. "One day my mom surprised me. I jumped up and down when I saw the pink bus for the first time. From the glitter on the ceiling to the huge mirror on the wall and the sign on the door that says 'Dance Street,' it is the most amazing thing ever."

Amiya's mobile dance studio takes off with her great uncle driving. When they get to a school, up to 12 kids pile on the bus for half-hour tap, ballet, and hip-hop lessons. The kids always tell Amiya how much they love dancing in the bus. And she loves teaching those kids. She calls them her rising stars.

Left: Amiya teaching ballet. Below: Her studio is inside an old school bus!

A Sister Act

Stepsisters Izzy M. and Madi D. love to dance—they dance in the studio, in their living room, and in shows all over their town. "My mom has a dance studio," says Madi, 11. "But instead of doing recitals, we do benefit shows." After each performance, the studio collects money from the audience to donate to good causes. The New York girls perform in many places, and they once danced in a Christmas show to raise money for a girl at their school who has cancer. So far, they have helped to raise $8,000.

"It feels great to help people by dancing," says Madi. Adds Izzy, who is also 11, "Getting ready for the benefits is fun. We put on makeup and costumes. We do jazz and modern dance—our whole family gets involved. I love to see all the people in the audience smiling."

Izzy and Madi

100 Pairs of Slippers

Drew B. loves ballet, so the 11-year-old Florida girl was interested to hear that lots of kids were taking ballet lessons at a local center. But when she found out that the kids were homeless and were dancing in socks instead of ballet shoes, "a lightbulb went on," she says. Drew and her mom, a volunteer dance instructor, made a plan to buy ballet shoes for the children.

Drew talked to neighbors, handed out flyers, and sent out e-[...] people she knew, raising about $2,000 in all. Then she and he[...] bought 100 pairs of new ballet slippers—black for the boys a[...] for the girls.

"When they saw the boxes, their faces glittered," Drew says. T[...] put on the shoes right away and started dancing. "They all tha[...] me. It made me feel wonderful," she says.

You can donate, too.

Have you outgrown the shoes you wear for dance class or a sport? If the shoes are in good shape, ask your dance teacher or coach about donating them to another kid who could use them.

Tutus for Charity

After her mom donated her own hair to an organization that makes wigs for cancer patients, Grace B. wanted to help, too. "I didn't have enough hair to donate," says Grace, "so I made and sold tutus to raise money for sick kids."

The Pennsylvania 8-year-old taught herself how to make tutus by researching online. "You unroll the tulle and cut it into strips," explains Grace, who loves color combinations such as purple, pink, and mermaid blue with sparkles. Next, she says, you sew the ends together and knot them around elastic.

With help from her mom, Grace created a website to sell the tutus. To celebrate her birthday, Grace donated a total of $500 to two children's hospitals.

"I feel happy when I wear a tutu," Grace says. "I want to change the world and be an inspiration for other kids."

About the Author

Laurence Yep is the author of more than 60 books. His numerous awards include two Newbery Honors and the Laura Ingalls Wilder medal for his contribution to children's literature. Several of his plays have been produced in New York, Washington, D.C., and California.

Though *The Nutcracker* was a regular holiday treat for Laurence as a boy, it was his wife, Joanne Ryder, who really showed him how captivating and inspiring dance can be with her gift of tickets to the San Francisco Ballet. Their seats were high in the balcony, yet they were able to see the graceful, expressive movements of the dancers far below.

Laurence Yep's books about Isabelle are his latest ones about ballet and a girl's yearning to develop her talents and become the dancer she so wishes to be.